ZO & ALANA

MICHELLE ELAINE

Cole Hart
SIGNATURE NOVELS

Zo & Alana

Copyright © 2020 by Michelle Elaine

All rights reserved.

Published in the United States of America.

Mailing List

To stay up to date on new releases, plus get information on contests, sneak peeks, and more,

Go To The Website Below...

www.colehartsignature.com

Cole Hart
SIGNATURE NOVELS

THANK YOU

To our loyal Cole Hart Signature readers,

Cole Hart Signature is always growing and changing. Some of you have been following Cole Hart since the beginning of his career, while others have seen us go from Cole Hart Presents to Cole Hart Signature. Then there are our daily new supporters who've only known us for what we are as a company today. Despite our changes, how or when you became a fanatic, we want to kindly thank you for the support.

We appreciate all our Cole Hart Readers because without every single one of you, we wouldn't be the company we are today.

If this book is your first introduction to our company, welcome! And be sure to sign up for email list by click the link, http://bit. ly/2BtGCXH, and joining out text-mail list by texting Cole-HartSig to (855)231-5230. Cole Hart Signature also has a Facebook group where fans get to discuss the plot, characters, overall releases about their favorite book. If itching for new and interesting conversation, click the link, https://geni.us/ ColeHartSignatureRead, to join today!

Lastly, Cole Hart Signature is always interested in partnering with aspiring authors, new or experienced, who thrive in the African Urban Fiction and Romance Fiction genre. If you're interested in joining our team, go to www.colehartsignature.com/submissions.

Once again, we truly appreciate all the support over the years.

Much Love,
   CHS

ALANA

"Uh uh, girl ... I know he didn't say that to you," my best friend, Porsha James, said while I held my cell phone up to my ear.

"Yeah. He did. I'm straight on the disrespect," I said, shaking my head. "As long as I've known him ... as much as we've been through together ... he's out his damn mind talking to me like that."

I sat on the edge of my tub while it filled with hot water. I dropped a bath bomb in and watched it fizz while Porsha and I continued to talk about my latest argument with my boyfriend. I heard the phone beep and looked down at the screen to see that he was calling me again, but I had nothing to say to him. Even if I did have something I wanted to say, it was way too late, and I was much too tired for our conversation. I looked at the screen until his name disappeared, and then I put the phone back up to my ear.

"Girl, he just tried to call me again," I said, rolling my eyes.

Porsha sighed. "La, maybe you just need to answer him. You know he's not going to stop," she said. "Also, it's late, and I have to work in the morning. Call me tomorrow."

We ended the call right as the phone started to vibrate in my hand.

Again.

I let it go to voicemail.

Again.

I rolled my eyes and shut off the running water. Standing up, I sat my phone down on the edge of the huger soaker tub before taking off my robe and slipping into the inviting bath. Porsha was right. It was late – well after one o'clock in the morning, and I had to work the next morning as well. However, it had been a long day, and I needed to unwind before climbing into my California King. I rested my head against my bath pillow and shut my eyes. A few moments later, I heard the short buzzing sound of my phone vibrating from a voicemail. That brought the grand total up to fifteen missed calls, eight text messages, and five voicemails – in the last hour. I was beyond annoyed. I knew the next time the phone rang one of three things was going to happen. I was either going to shut the phone off completely, throw it across the room, or ...

"*What?*" I yelled as I angrily answered the ringing phone.

He didn't say anything. I only heard him sigh heavily ... and then nothing but the sound of the steadily falling rain outside in the background. I was not in the mood for his shit.

"Dammit, you've been calling me all night long. You've got another three seconds to say something before I hang up and turn off this phone."

"Lala, I'm outside."

"*What?*"

"I'm outside the door," he said. He sighed again. "I ain't know you had the locks changed. Look ... I know you're mad, baby ... and I don't blame you. Just let me in for a minute. I promise I ain't even trying to stay. For real, babe ... I'm standing out here getting rained on and shit ... rain coming down all sideways ... La, please. Just let me in."

I hung up. For a moment, I just sat in the tub with the phone in my hand. I didn't tell him to drive thirty minutes across town in the middle of a storm. Like he said, he knew I had good reason to be upset with him. We had been having the same argument for weeks ... months even. There were no signs of things getting better. In fact, they were getting worse, and I was tired. I didn't want to argue. I didn't want to fight. I didn't want to talk to him, see him, or listen to any more excuses. My better judgement was urging me to settle back into my bath and close my eyes. The voice in my head was telling me to turn the phone off and ignore him, but I knew he would kick the door in if he really wanted to get inside my home.

Besides, my heart was telling me to do something totally different.

I pushed myself up to my feet and stepped onto my bath rug. I grabbed my towel and quickly dried myself off. Grabbing a short nightgown from my dresser, I slipped it over my head and rushed to my window. Looking down at the driveway, I saw his Range Rover. He was actually on my damn porch. I raced down the steps and swung the front door open before I even had a chance to think clearly. We stood facing each other in silence for a few seconds before he spoke.

"Damn, babe. You gonna let me in or what?"

"What the hell did you come over here for?" I snapped. "You know that I have to work in the morning."

He shook his head and released a frustrated sigh. "Come on, La. Let me in."

I only hesitated briefly before stepping to the side and letting him into the house. He walked past me into the foyer, leaving me to close and lock the door. He was soaking wet – dripping water all over my hardwood floors.

"You're getting my floors wet," I said, evenly as I leaned against the front door.

"Floors that I paid for," he responded quickly. "Floors you know I can pay to replace with no issue."

I shook my head and laughed. "That's not the point."

With a hint of attitude, he asked, "Then what is your point?"

I hesitated for a moment but ultimately chose to ignore his tone of voice. I was trying to learn how to choose my battles when it came to him. So, I purposely ignored the way he was speaking to me in my house.

"What do you want?" I calmly asked instead.

"What do you mean what do I want?" he asked, slipping out of his jacket and hanging it on the doorknob of the coat closet.

I wondered why he was taking his jacket off and getting comfortable if he supposedly wasn't trying and stay. However, I was also distracted by the tattoo-covered, well-defined muscles in his arms that were exposed by the short-sleeved T-shirt he wore.

"Why are you here right now?"

"Because I wanted to see you. I wanted to apologize about earlier."

"You said you were sorry in one of the many text messages you sent. I get it ... you're sorry – sorry as hell," I said. "That still doesn't answer why you came all the way over here ... or how you even got out of the house?"

His face twisted into a frown.

"What?"

"I mean ... how did you slip out unnoticed? What did your wife have to say about you creeping out of the house in the middle of the night?" I asked, folding my arms across my chest.

He hated when I mentioned his wife, but we had been tiptoeing around the elephant in the room for far too long. Given our circumstances, there was no way for me to avoid mentioning her. With his fists clenched and jaw tight, he crossed the foyer until he was standing right in front of me.

"I think you forgot how shit runs over there. I pay the bills in that damn house," he said. "She doesn't tell me what to do, and she sure as hell doesn't tell me when I can come and go."

He intimidated a lot of people, but I wasn't one of them. Not anymore anyway. We were way past that. He was a good six feet three inches tall and about two hundred and forty solid pounds of cinnamon brown perfection. He towered over my five-foot three-inch, hundred and fifty-pound frame. I rolled my eyes and shoved past him, heading into my kitchen. Since I was still awake and dealing with his bullshit, I figured I might as well have a drink. I grabbed a wine glass out of a nearby cabinet and poured half a glass of merlot. He followed me into the kitchen and leaned against the dishwasher.

"No. I'm fine. Don't bother getting me anything to drink," he said with sarcasm.

I slammed my hand down on the granite countertop and turned around to face him. "Dammit, Zo! If you came here to be an asshole, you can get back in your car and go home."

He covered his face with his hands and let out a deep sigh while I guzzled down half of my wine. Dropping his hands by his side, he looked into my face while I sat the glass back down on the counter.

"Alana, I don't know what to say," he said, shrugging his shoulders.

"Okay ... I don't know what you should say either," I said. "So why don't you leave me alone, and go home to your wife?"

"Because I'm where I want to be!" he shouted. I raised an eyebrow at him, silently questioning if he had lost his mind. He lowered his tone of voice before speaking to me again. "If I wanted to be with her, don't you think I would be over there right now instead of standing here arguing with you? Babe, just give me some more time ... I'm going to handle all of that. I swear."

I shook my head as I stared into his eyes.

"You're going to *handle all of that*? Yeah okay," I said sarcastically. "You've had plenty of time to do something if you really wanted. How much longer do you think I can go on like this?"

"I know at this point everything I say probably sounds like an excuse, but ... you know where my heart is," he said. "You know that I love you. If you don't believe anything else that I say, you need to believe that."

I just looked at him. I knew that he loved me. We loved each other. However, I was starting to feel like love wasn't enough.

"Alana, if I could do it all over again, I never would have chosen her. You know you're the one, La," he said, as he walked back over to me. He slid his arms around my waist, pulling my body against his. "Baby, I told you that I'm going to make things right for us. You just gotta be patient. I'm just asking you to give me a little bit more time. You know that you're the one I want to come home to every night."

"Stop it!" I shouted as I tried to push him away. He barely moved. "Stop trying to tell me that I'm the one you want to be with. Stop coming over here trying to fill my head up with your bullshit. Quit trying to sell me dreams. You're a grown ass man, Lorenzo. You've made it quite clear that you do what you want. If you wanted to leave her, you would have done it already. You've had plenty of time to do it."

Zo sighed, and I pulled away from him.

"Wait a minute," he said, reaching for me in an attempt to calm me down.

I slapped his hands away and shoved him hard in his rock-solid chest – pushing him less than six inches away from me.

"No," I refused. "You stand here and tell me that I'm the one you want to come home to, but the fact of the matter is that I'm not. Courtney's probably sound asleep in your bed while I'm fighting with you at two o'clock in the morning. I swear sometimes I don't even know what I'm doing anymore."

"Don't say that, La. You know what we're doing," he said, as he reached for me again.

"Come here."

I shook my head and pushed him away.

"Come ... here," he repeated more forcefully, grabbing my arm.

I didn't resist. I probably should have stopped him when he

grabbed the back of my neck and pressed his lips against mine, but I didn't. Zo was naturally charismatic and downright sexy as hell. It didn't take much for me to cave. Even when he made me mad as hell, my body still responded to him. It was like he cast some sort of spell on me. I tried to pick and choose my battles with him, but this wasn't something I could fight. I knew it was wrong. Our entire relationship was wrong, but that didn't stop me. The reality of our situation didn't make me resist his firm grip on my waist when he lifted me onto the kitchen island. I should have stopped him when his hands traveled up my legs, rubbing my thighs. I should have stopped him when he started to kiss on my neck and undo his jeans.

But I didn't.

Zo pressed his full lips into the crook of my neck – licking and sucking – while he pushed my nightgown up around my waist, my bare ass sitting on the cold granite of the kitchen island. I pulled his shirt over his head and placed my hands on his shoulders to steady myself as he lowered his jeans and underwear down around his knees. With one hand, he pushed my knee to spread my legs wider. With the other hand, he stroked himself before sliding his way inside of me. I gasped before releasing a deep, throaty moan. I had never gotten used to his size. He grabbed my waist, pulling me closer to the edge of the counter while he forcefully delivered slow and steady strokes.

The kitchen island provided balance, but I still leaned into him. I wrapped my legs around his waist and my arms around his torso. I pressed my forehead against his chest, closing my eyes and biting my bottom lip.

"You still mad at me?" he asked.

"Yes."

He shook his head at me. "For real, La?"

I didn't respond. Zo gripped my waist tighter and increased his pace, driving into me much faster than he had moments earlier. Grabbing my ponytail, Zo pulled my head back and kissed me so deeply he took away what little breath I had.

7

"You sure you mad?"

"Yes," I cried.

Zo lifted me from the island. He turned around and pinned my back against the stainless-steel refrigerator, all while moving inside of me faster and harder. He kissed my neck again.

"You really mad at me, babe?"

Barely able to breathe, I didn't even try to open my mouth to speak. I wrapped my arms around his neck and shook my head no.

"That's what I thought."

Gripping my thighs, Zo penetrated me deeper and deeper with each mind-numbing stroke. Panting breathlessly, I clawed at his back unconsciously digging my long-manicured nails into his skin. Minutes later, I felt his body stiffen while he started to throb and release inside of me. He held onto me tightly when his body slumped forward, and his forehead rested against the refrigerator. We were both trying to catch our breath. After a few moments, Zo stood up straight, lifted me off him, and placed me on my feet. I pulled my nightgown back down while he pulled his pants up.

"You still want me to leave?" he asked, zipping his jeans.

I shook my head and ran my hands over my hair, smoothing down my ponytail.

"Good," Zo laughed as he grabbed a bottle of water from the refrigerator. "I wasn't going anywhere anyway."

I rolled my eyes and shook my head while I placed my empty wine glass in the sink. Still laughing, Zo grabbed my arm and pulled me towards him.

"All bullshit aside you know I love you, Lala," he said in a serious tone.

"I know. I love you too."

With his hand under my chin, he raised my lips to meet his. He kissed me deeply and passionately before pulling away.

"Come on. Let's go upstairs."

. . .

NICK

"Here go your wings," the attractive waitress said after sitting the basket of hot wings and fries in front of me. She had to lean in so I could hear her clearly over the loud club music. She tucked her hair behind her ear and smiled at me seductively. "Can I get you anything else?"

I sat my beer down and returned her smile. "Yeah," I said, eyeing the curves of her body. "Your name and phone number."

With a shy laugh she picked up my cell phone and input her contact information. She mouthed 'call me' before walking off. I felt a hand on my shoulder and turned to see JB sitting down next to me.

"Man, I can't take your ass nowhere," JB laughed. "Now I see why you didn't bring Kayla out tonight."

I laughed and shook my head. "Nah. Kayla's out of town. If she was here, she wouldn't have a problem with me getting a few numbers," I said. "Hell, that waitress was Kayla's type too. We could have all had some fun tonight."

JB shook his head and reached for the nearest bottle of brown liquor. It was the end of a long week. It had been a very lucrative week, but man, did we have to work for it. Since taking over the trap that used to belong to Prime, I was working closely with JB. He was in charge of the muscle and making sure that things stayed safe and sound during the change of leadership. The last thing we needed was any problems that would make our business the lead story on the eleven o'clock news.

My big brother, Zo, had gone out on a limb for me by giving me my own spot. We had been working with PO for years, but this was the first time I was given a position of leadership. Ordinarily managing anything or anyone other than myself was not my thing, but a bigger role meant more money in my pockets. If anyone knew anything about me, they knew I loved money. I wasn't going to ruin the opportunity. My brother had trusted me with something important for once. I didn't want to make him

9

regret it. In addition to the faith Zo had in me, PO made certain promises to the mayor. I didn't want to let him down either.

Without PO, Zo and I never would have gotten our start in the streets. Zo and I went to school with Alana Woods and her older brother, Marcus. Their uncle Darrell, who was best friends with PO and worked for Julian Reid's organization for years, raised them. When Marcus and Alana both showed interest in making some money Darrell got PO to ask Julian for approval. Julian initially had reservations about it, because they were young. However, at PO's urging, he relented. Once Marcus and Alana got on, they got Zo and me in as well. Throughout the years, we had all remained close. Even with Marcus locked up for the past few years, he and Zo were still best friends.

My phone buzzed while I enjoyed my hot wings. I glanced at the screen and saw that my sister in law, Courtney, was calling me. I sighed and shook my head. I quickly decided to let her call go to voicemail. If she was calling me this late at night, it probably had something to do with my brother, and I was in too good of a mood to be in the middle of their mess. I was dipping a second flat in ranch when Courtney called me again. I sighed even heavier. She was relentless. If she was really trying to get ahold of me, I knew she wouldn't give up without trying at least twenty times.

I sat my wing down and wiped my hands before picking up the phone.

"Hold on Court ... let me get somewhere I can hear you."

I asked JB to watch my stuff while I walked towards the hallway leading to the men's room. The music was obscenely loud, so I stepped inside the bathroom and pressed the phone back up to my ear.

"What's going on?"

"Where the hell is your brother?" she demanded. "I've been trying to reach him for over an hour."

I shook my head. I was annoyed that once again, I was being pulled into the middle of their drama.

"I don't know, Court. If he ain't answering his phone, he's probably busy."

"Don't bullshit me, Nick. You two have been joined at the hip lately, but now all of a sudden you want me to believe that you don't know where he is?"

I hesitated before lying to her again. The truth was that even though I hadn't spoken to my brother in hours, I had a pretty good idea of where he was. To the best of my knowledge, he didn't have anything work-related going on that night. So, if it was after two in the morning and his wife couldn't find him, he was probably with his other woman, Alana Woods. We had all been close friends since middle and high school. Alana and Zo engaged in harmless flirting for years before becoming romantically involved three years prior – right after Marcus went to prison. A number of people were aware of their involvement, but Courtney obviously wasn't one of them.

"Look Court, I don't know what he's got going on, but I'll try to get ahold of him," I answered. "If he –"

"When you talk to him, tell him that Bryson has a high-grade fever, and he's been throwing up all night," she said, cutting me off. "We're at Children's Healthcare if he gives a shit."

Before I could ask any questions, Courtney hung up the phone. I typically tried to stay out of Zo's shit when it came to his messy ass love life. However, I knew that regardless of his drama with his wife, he loved his kids. Whether he was laid up with Alana or just ignoring Courtney's calls as he often did, I knew he would want to know that one of his six-year-old twin boys was at the hospital. I dialed his phone number, but he didn't answer for me either. I sent him a text to inform him of the situation and put my phone in my pocket. I left the bathroom and headed back to my wings.

I had done my due diligence. Zo could handle everything else whenever he decided to answer his phone.

2
ZO

When my eyes opened, I picked my watch up from Alana's bedside table and saw that it was a little after seven in the morning. I didn't get nearly enough sleep. However, Alana had to be at work soon, and I figured I would leave the house when she did. I sat my watch back down and reached for my phone, but it wasn't there. Pushing the covers back on the bed, I sat up and felt around in the sheets. It wasn't in the bed either. Hearing the running water of the shower, I walked over to the cracked door of the master bathroom. I pushed it all the way open.

"Babe, you seen my phone?"

"No," Alana answered. "You didn't bring it upstairs. It's probably in your jacket."

I left the bathroom and jogged down the steps to the coat closet, where my jacket was hanging on the doorknob. I felt around in the pockets before retrieving my phone. It was rare that my phone was not within arm's reach. When I looked at my notifications, it was obvious why I always kept it so close. I had several missed calls and texts. I had the most missed calls from Courtney, but I there were also missed notifications from Nick, PO, and a few other business associates. My eyes landed on a text message from my brother, informing me that Courtney was at the hospital with one of our sons.

I tried to call him back, but he didn't answer. I hung up and dialed my wife's number. She picked up on the first ring.

"Where the fuck are you?"

I ignored her question and asked one of my own. "Is Bryson okay?"

"We're back at home if that's what you're wondering," she responded. "Doctor said they think it was just a 24-hour bug. He's sleeping now, and I've got Brandon in another room, so he doesn't get sick too."

"Alright. I'm on my way home."

"For what?"

"What you mean?"

"What you coming home for now, Zo?" Courtney asked. "I took care of everything like I always do."

"Because that's my damn house and those are my kids."

I hung up the phone and started back up the stairs. When I re-entered the bedroom, Alana was fresh out of the shower with a towel wrapped around her curvaceous body. I paused for a moment to admire her appearance. Alana had a flawlessly smooth complexion the color of milk chocolate and thick black hair pulled into a ponytail on top of her head. Her round face captured the attention of many men with her round cheeks, almond-shaped up-turned eyes, and full pouty lips. She was petite in height only. The shape of her body was what most people would call thick. Her curves were one of my favorite things about her physical appearance. She did a good job of keeping her body toned and her waist tight, but she still had big breasts, thick thighs, and a fat ass. I subconsciously grabbed my crotch, readjusting myself. Neither one of us had time for the things I wanted to do.

"You got a long day at work?"

Alana shook her head. "Just an early start. I should probably be done around three."

Alana pulled her ponytail loose allowing her hair to flow down her back before she snatched her towel off and tossed it onto her bed. Again, she had my full attention. I watched her naked body move across the room to her dresser, where she pulled on her bra and underwear. She was rubbing on lotion before I spoke again.

"I have to head out, but I'll hit you up later," I said, picking my jeans up from the floor.

"Okay."

Alana rubbed the last of her lotion into her skin and walked over to me. I finished pulling my shirt on, and she wrapped her arms around my waist to hug me tightly. I kissed her lips and softly grabbed her behind before we pulled away from our embrace.

"I'm not leaving for another thirty minutes so lock up for me on your way out," she said, returning to her dresser to grab clothes for the day.

I nodded. "Speaking of locking up," I said, stepping into my shoes. "You gonna give me a new key?"

Alana paused at her open drawer and looked at me over her shoulder. "Do you think that I should?"

"My name is on the deed to this house just like yours," I answered. "I've had a key since you got keys, but you got mad and changed the locks on a house that I paid for. Come on, La. You tell me."

Alana pulled on a shirt and slammed her drawer closed. She turned around to face me. "For real, Zo? You also paid for my car. Do you want the spare key to that too? I never would have agreed to any of this if I knew you were going to throw it in my face. You said you were just making sure I was straight while Marcus was away. I should've known better."

Alana shook her head and walked away from me in the direction of her closet. I sighed heavily. I needed to get home to check on my son and check in with Courtney, but I didn't want to leave with Alana still mad at me. I came over the night before to stop the arguing and petty drama that had gone on between us for a few days. I followed her into the closet to find her opening and closing drawers in her jewelry organizer. She threw a key at me that hit me in the chest before falling to the ground.

"Here's your damn key."

She turned her back towards me and grabbed a pair of jeans off a hanger. I picked the key off the floor, sliding it in my pocket while she tugged on her pants. I walked over to her and tried to pull her into my arms. She pushed me away.

"Bye Lorenzo."

I smirked and shook my head at her attitude. She only called me by my full name when she was mad. By this point, I was familiar with her behavior. Since her brother was one of my best friends, I had always been close with Alana. However, our relationship had really grown over the last couple of years.

"Alright, Lala. I'll call you later."

I kissed her on the forehead and left her alone in her closet. I grabbed my jacket on the way out and was in my truck in a matter of moments. I pulled out of Alana's driveway and started the drive over to the house I shared with Courtney.

I didn't think it was possible for the two women in my life to be any more different.

Several years prior, I met Courtney at a gas station. Her face caught my attention while I was trying to fill up my car. We exchanged numbers and started a whirlwind relationship that quickly led to marriage and kids. Without ever discussing it directly, her parents always had an idea of what I did for a living, which was why they never supported us. Their lack of support led to a quickie courthouse wedding and the absence of her parents at the hospital when our twins were born. As someone who was always close with their parents, I felt sorry for her. That was until I realized that she cared more about the things I could give her than she actually cared about me. Courtney accused me of being unfaithful long before I ever became involved with Alana. Our relationship had been rocky for almost five years. I assumed that the main reason she stayed was because she had grown too accustomed to the lifestyle I provided her. Courtney didn't give a shit about me. She didn't want to lose the house, clothes, and cars.

I had known Alana since I was a fifteen-year-old freshman in high school. At the time, I only knew her as the younger sister of the guy who eventually became my best friend. Through the years, we all got closer due to the time we spent working for Julian Reid – the number one drug distributor in Atlanta, and his right-hand man, PO. Several years later, when her cosmetology career was close to taking off and she considered leaving the streets behind, I started to see her in a different light. A light that I wasn't sure her older brother, my best friend Marcus, would approve. After a while of flirting back and forth, we crossed the line to something more than friendship the night she celebrated her twenty-fifth birthday – shortly after Marcus went to prison. Despite my marital status, it didn't take long for Alana to capture my heart. We had our ups and downs, but I would move heaven and earth for her. The words I told her were true. If I could do it all over again, I would have chosen her.

I just had to figure out the best way to handle Courtney.

I pulled into the garage and shut the engine off. I sat in the truck for a few moments to get my mind right before I entered the house. I knew I was going to have to deal with drama from Courtney. There was always drama with Courtney, even before things became physical with Alana. Courtney wasn't familiar with the streets like the rest of us. In all the time we had been together, she still didn't seem to understand. She didn't understand that all the material things she loved so much came at a price. I was never going to be the PTA dad that had a nine to five and was home for dinner every night. That would never be me.

I exited my truck and entered my house. Courtney was sitting at the kitchen island with a cup of coffee and her cell phone.

"Hey."

"Hey," she said without looking up at me.

"Are the boys sleep?"

"Yeah. They were up most of the night."

Courtney took a sip of her coffee and continued to look down at her phone. I paused for a moment. I was expecting a full-on rant from Courtney or a shouting match about how I didn't come home the night before. That's what I was used to. The cold shoulder she was giving me was new. I wasn't sure what was the reason behind her change in demeanor, but I was grateful to avoid an argument. I turned to leave the kitchen.

"So that's it?"

I was halfway across the room but paused when I heard Courtney's voice. I sighed heavily and turned around to face my wife.

"What?"

Courtney stood up from her stool with her arms folded across her chest.

"You don't have anything to say about last night?"

"What do you want me to say, Court?"

"Something. You didn't respond to any of my texts or calls last night. I had to have your brother reach out to you, and you still didn't call me back until this morning. What the hell, Zo? I had to take our child to the emergency room last night, and you were nowhere to be found."

I shrugged my shoulders. "Look, I'm sorry about that. I didn't have my phone on me, but I'm here now."

"For how long?" Courtney asked. "You're so damn predictable. You're probably about to head upstairs and check on the boys, take a shower, and head right back out. You'll tell me you've got work to do, but you're probably going to end up with whatever bitch you spent the night with."

There it was. Courtney always went there. During the course of any argument, she would always bring up infidelity or complain about me working all the time. Most of the time, she would complain about both. I just stared at her and shook my head. She was the predictable one.

"Alright Court," I said, turning back towards the stairs.

Courtney rushed in front of me, standing in my way while I tried to climb the steps.

"What?" I asked in a frustrated tone.

"I don't want you to disturb the boys. They were up all night, and they need to rest," she said.

I shrugged my shoulders.

"Okay. I'll see them later."

"Actually, we're going to Charlotte to visit my sister for fall break. We'll be leaving this afternoon."

"Alright," I responded nonchalantly.

I gently moved Courtney to the side and continued up the stairs. Regardless of her request, I went to check on my sons. After spending a few minutes with them, I laid down for a quick nap heading back out for work. I hated that the boys were leaving town, but I was relieved to get a break from Courtney.

PO

"Looks like another good week is almost in the books," Aaron Mercer said.

"Pretty much," I said, holding my cell phone up to my ear. "Some of the guys have already dropped off their split. I'm about to ride over to Nick's trap in a minute to check things out over there before we collect the rest of the money tonight."

"How's everything working out with Nick?"

I looked out the window of the office at the car wash I owned. Zo and JB were out front shooting the shit and cleaning their cars. To be completely honest, Zo's younger brother had far exceeded my expectations. I had known the men since they were young boys. One of my best friends, Darrell Woods, and I spent years working for Julian Reid. Darrell raised his sister's kids, Alana and Marcus Woods, due to their mother's drug addiction and instability. Darrell never hid his involvement in the business from the kids, so it was no surprise that they eventually showed interest in working with Julian's team to make money for themselves. Marcus and Alana were friends with Zo and Nick and eventually brought them into the fold as well. After Darrell was killed ten years ago, I made it my business to personally look out for all of them.

Zo, Nick, and Marcus all started out as corner boys but ended up taking different paths. While Zo's intellect and ruthlessness propelled him to be my right hand, Nick was comfortable as a street level dealer for a long time. I was surprised by both his performance over the last couple of months and the fact that he even wanted to be in a position that required more responsibility. I was looking forward to seeing him develop. Marcus was currently locked up on drugs and weapon charges. He had always been a troublemaker and a hot head. Prior to his incarceration, he was an enforcer on the streets. If he was a free man, he would have been in charge of the muscle – instead of JB. Marcus's younger sister, Alana, worked for the team for a few years as well. A few years back, she realized that she wanted to do something different with her life, and Marcus paid to send her to cosmetology school. Even though she wasn't connected to the business anymore, she was still pretty close with my family.

I brought my thoughts back to my conversation with Aaron, who had recently taken over as the head of the Ramirez Cartel due to his father's failing health.

"Nick has really stepped it up. I never thought he would want to run anything, but he's exceeded my expectations for sure," I said.

"Turns out Zo knew what he was talking about, huh?" Aaron asked.

"He typically does."

Zo had always had an eye for the business, and he rarely let personal feelings or relationships interfere. When he said Nick was ready for a bigger role, I trusted that his decision was based on Nick's desire and capabilities – not his familial relationship.

"That's what's up," Aaron said. "Man, you don't know how relieved I am to hear that things are going so smoothly up there. I ain't trying to be in Atlanta any time soon."

We both laughed. After facing a number of threats to our business, Aaron ended up spending a considerable amount of time in Atlanta. That was how he met and married his wife, Jada, the younger daughter of the late Julian Reid. Aaron was born and raised in Miami, and Jada had recently relocated there to have their family all under the same roof.

"Shit, I'm relieved too," I said. "My plan is to keep things going like this, so you don't have to be back up here anytime soon."

"Sounds good to me, man. I'mma let you go on and finish handling your business. I've got something to do with Jada and the kids, but if you need anything just let me or Luke know," he said, referring to his best friend, Lucas Malone.

"Bet."

I ended the call and looked back out the window to see the men were finishing up with their vehicles. I exited the building and approached them while looking at my watch.

"Hey, I'm trying to roll over to Nick's spot, grab something to eat, and be back here before five," I said. "Y'all ready to ride?"

They nodded and climbed into my truck before I took off towards Nick's location. Soon we made it to our destination to check in on his set-up. As expected, everything was running smoothly. After spending a little over an hour there, Zo and I decided to grab lunch while JB hung back with Nick's crew. Nick walked outside with us, following us to my truck.

"What y'all got going on tonight?" Nick asked.

"After we wrap up business for the day, I'm headed home," I answered. "We're going to see Aisha at school tomorrow."

My oldest daughter was a freshman at Georgia Southern University.

"What about you?" Nick asked his brother.

Zo shrugged his shoulders. "Not sure. Court's taking the boys to visit her sister, but I might have some other plans."

I quietly smirked at Zo's response. I knew that his *other plans* probably included Alana. He and I rarely spoke about it directly, but their relationship was a poorly kept secret around our circle. It seemed like the only people who didn't know about their relationship was his wife and her brother. I knew Zo had genuine feelings for Alana. I just wished he would end things with his wife if he no longer wanted to be in the marriage. Alana deserved much more than being some man's other woman.

"Yeah alright," Nick laughed. "If your *other plans* fall through, let me know. We're probably going to Blaze."

"Alright," Zo laughed.

A car pulled up to the house, stopping at the bottom of the driveway. People came and went all the time, so I wasn't too concerned. I continued my conversation with Nick and Zo, figuring that the man walking up the driveway was headed into the house. That was until he stopped a few yards away from where we stood.

"Aye man ... you're PO, right?"

Nick and Zo frowned at him.

I hesitated before responding. "Who's asking?"

The man smirked before reaching behind him and quickly pulling a gun from his waistband. Nick, Zo, and I all pulled our weapons, but the other man started shooting first. One of us struck him in the arm as he ran back to the waiting vehicle. Nick chased after the car, shooting at them until they were out of range. I looked over towards Zo, who was grabbing at his left arm.

"Fuck!" he shouted. Blood was seeping through his fingers. "What the fuck was that?"

Zo turned to look at me, and I watched as his eyes quickly widened.

"PO!" he called my name. "You're hit, man."

I frowned in confusion, but then I felt the pain. I felt a pain so breathtaking and overwhelming that it brought me to my knees. I looked down to see blood leaking from my wounds, slowly but surely soaking my shirt.

I started to feel lightheaded.

Zo and Nick rushed over to me, and I heard sounds that sounded like them speaking to me. However, their voices were muffled. The voices sounded further away than they should have been. I blinked hard, and my vision was starting to blur. Then I felt my body fall face forward towards the pavement right as my eyes closed.

❧ 3 ❧

ALANA

I walked my last client to the door and then returned to my station. I was ready to go home. I desperately needed a nap if I was going to do anything besides sleep that night. I put up my tools and swept the floor. Satisfied that my area was clean, I grabbed my purse. After saying goodbye to a few of the other stylists, I was walking towards the front door when Ayanna Reid-Carter called my name.

I stopped and turned around to answer the shop owner. Both daughters of the late Julian Reid, Ayanna and her sister Jada, opened the salon almost two years earlier. At the time, I was working at another popular salon in Buckhead, but Julian recommended me to his daughters. I happily joined their team. Even though I had not worked for him in a few years, Julian always looked out for me. He was just that type of man.

"Hey Yanni. What's up?" I asked, walking over to her.

"Are you headed out for a late lunch, or are you finished for the day?" she asked.

"I am done until Tuesday morning," I answered with a smile.

"Do you have a quick minute?" she asked. "I'd like to speak with you about something."

"Sure."

23

Ayanna motioned for me to follow her to her office. When we entered the nicely decorated space, she closed the door before we took our seats. We rarely had closed door meetings, so I wondered what was going on. I was one of the more popular stylists in the shop with a list of high-profile clients. I never brought any issues or drama to work. I was a model employee.

"Since you were on your way out, I'm going to get right to the point," Ayanna said with a smile.

I relaxed at the sight of her pleasant demeanor. At least I wasn't in any type of trouble.

"You know my sister has recently moved to Miami and turned the business completely over to me ..."

I nodded. I ran into Jada before she left town. I knew that she had moved to Miami to be with her young son and husband, Aaron Mercer – the head of the Ramirez Cartel.

"Yeah. I know."

"She also left me in charge of her restaurant and boutique in Buckhead," Ayanna said. "It's kind of hard to be in three places at once, so I'm looking for someone to help me out around here."

I raised an eyebrow.

"When my dad recommended you, he said that you had an incredible work ethic, and you have definitely demonstrated that during your time here," she said. "So, I wanted to discuss a new role with you."

"New role?"

"Yes. I know you love being a stylist and working with your clients, but I am wondering how you would feel about management. Is that something you might be interested in?"

I smiled and nodded. "Yes. Very interested."

"Good," Ayanna said, sliding a piece of paper in front of me. "Then the job is yours. Here's an official offer letter. It comes with a base salary. Annual booth rent has already been deducted from the salary offer figuring you still want to see clients. So, any money you make from doing hair is completely yours. Will this number suffice?"

My eyes traveled down to the number Ayanna pointed to on the offer letter and widened with surprise. Pleasant surprise.

"Oh my God. Yes! Thank you."

"You are welcome. You have been such an asset to the team here. It hasn't gone unnoticed," Ayanna said handing me a pen.

I signed the offer letter and handed both it and the pen back to my boss.

"Great. Enjoy the rest of your weekend, Lala," Ayanna said, standing up and shaking my hand. "See you Tuesday morning. I'll have your office ready for you when you get here."

I said goodbye and practically skipped out of the salon. I was unlocking the doors to my white BMW X6 when my phone started to vibrate in my bag. I grabbed the phone right as I slid behind the wheel of my ride. My face lit up when I saw Zo's name on the screen. Even though I was still mad at him when he left my house that morning, I couldn't wait to share my good news.

"Baby, I was just about to call you."

"Lala, it's me ... Nick."

I pulled the phone away from my ear to check the screen again. Nick was calling me from Zo's phone. Why? For some reason my stomach instantly became unsettled.

"Nick? Nick! What's going on? Why are you calling me from Zo's phone?"

"I dropped mine and messed it up at ... look ... something happened, La."

"Something like what? Where is your brother?"

My heart started racing and pounding so loudly I could feel it in my ears. I didn't like the sound of Nick's voice. He sounded as unsettled as I felt.

"There was a shooting at my spot. PO and Zo –"

"PO and Zo what?" I demanded.

"They got hit."

My hand flew to my chest. "Nick, is he ... is he ..."

"Zo's fine, La. Maybe just a graze ... but PO ... it's bad, Lala. Real bad. I think you might want to get to Grady. I'm here with them now."

"I'm on my way."

I put my car in drive and practically flew to Grady Memorial Hospital. I parked in the first spot I could find and quickly hopped out of my car. Sprinting towards the emergency entrance, I moved at lightning speed only slowing down when I approached Courtney, Zo's wife, as she stepped outside of the door.

She briefly looked at me with surprise but then quickly forced a weak smile onto her face and gave me a loose hug. "Alana ... hey."

"Hey Courtney," I greeted her. "Nick told me that PO's kind of bad off. I got over here as soon as I could."

I purposely didn't mention her husband.

"Yeah," she said with a somber look on her face. "It doesn't look good at all. He might be in surgery for a while."

There was a brief, awkward silence between us. Courtney was aware that Zo and I had been friends for a long time, but she never really accepted me as a part of his life. She wasn't thrilled that he had a female best friend. Given the true nature of my relationship with her husband, I couldn't blame Courtney for her lack of warmth towards me.

"Nick is in the waiting room. They're patching Zo up, but he should be cleared soon. In case you were wondering ..."

"Thanks. I appreciate the info. I'll check on them as well," I said. "Are you leaving?"

Courtney nodded. "Yeah. I just came by to make sure that Zo was fine," she answered. "I've got to hit the road. I'm taking the boys to Charlotte."

I nodded and nervously fumbled with the shoulder strap of my designer handbag. "Oh. Well ... I'm going to head inside. Take care, Courtney."

"You too."

Courtney headed for her car while I rushed inside the hospital. I found Nick inside of the waiting room, pacing back and forth with Zo's cell phone pressed to his ear. I quickly made my way over to him, hugging him tightly. Nick ended the call and wrapped his arms around my shoulders.

"It's going to be okay," he said to me. "It has to be."

I nodded, but I wasn't so sure. On the phone Nick made Zo's injury sound minimal, but I knew I would be concerned until I laid eyes on him. This wasn't the first time he had been shot. A couple years ago, Zo was injured during the middle of Julian Reid's battle with Caleb Bridges and KS9. He had taken a bullet to the leg the same night that Kelvin Massey was killed in a shooting at the now closed club, Passions.

Nick and I sat side by side in the waiting room while we waited for Zo. We waited for the better part of an hour during which time PO's longtime girlfriend, Kiara, arrived. We greeted Kiara and sat near her while we all continued to wait. A little later, Zo slowly made his way into the busy waiting room, eyes darting around until they landed on us. My stomach turned at the amount of blood on his shirt. His left sleeve was rolled up, displaying a large bandaged area on his upper arm. I quickly hopped to my feet and ran over to him. He wrapped his uninjured arm around me, embracing me tightly before kissing my forehead.

"I'm okay, La," he said. "I'm okay, but ..."

Zo stopped speaking and pulled away from me. He walked over to Kiara and squatted down in front of her. He spoke to her quietly – so quietly that I couldn't make out what he was saying. However, I saw the look on her face. I knew what was happening before it happened a few moments later. I just didn't want to accept it. PO was the closest thing I had to a father figure since my Uncle Darrell was killed. I had done Kiara and their daughters' hair for years. We spent holidays together. With Marcus in prison, they, Zo, and Nick were the only family I had. A couple more seconds passed before the two doctors walked into the waiting room looking for Kiara. Zo went with her when the doctors pulled her to the side to deliver the news – the news I knew Zo had unofficially shared with her already.

My thoughts were confirmed when I heard Kiara's cries moments later.

PO was dead.

ZO

I rested my head on my pillow while I watched Alana's wind her hips, her body rising and falling on top of mine. I was mesmerized by her shape as I took in my view. I kept my hands on her waist while she spread her thick thighs even further, taking me in even deeper. Her breasts bounced with each movement, and I was deep in a trance. There were several things I loved about Alana's body – including a number of tattoos with one being a half sleeve on her right arm. She also had a couple of tattoos that were only visible with her clothes off. One of those tattoos being the matching crown tattoo that we shared – mine on my chest and hers on her hip.

Alana threw her head back while she continued to ride me. Her eyes were closed, and her mouth hung open while she moaned loudly. I gripped her waist tighter and started to control her movements, bring her down onto me faster and harder. When Alana leaned forward, her breasts brushed against my chest while one of her hands gripped my shoulder and the other hand caressed the side of my face, stroking my beard. I touched a wall inside of her, reaching a place where I couldn't go any deeper.

"Damn baby," she whimpered in my ear before resting her head next to mine and kissing my neck.

I felt her body tremble, and her thighs clench around my waist. Like usual, I brought her to the peak of satisfaction. I slid my hands from her waist to her ass, grabbing it firmly. I continued to pound into her until a familiar tingle coursed through my body triggering my release as well. I kissed the top of Alana's head, and she laid on top of me until we caught our breaths. I felt a wetness on my shoulder and discovered its source when Alana sat up, and I saw tears on her cheeks. I looked at her with concern and touched the side of her face, using my thumb to wipe the tears from her face.

"Babe ... you good?"

Alana started to shake her head, but then she nodded instead. "I'm fine," she said, quickly rolling off me. "We need to start getting ready, so we're not late. I'mma hop in the shower."

Alana hopped up and rushed into the bedroom. Confused, I sat up in the bed and leaned against the headboard. I heard the shower running and decided to join her. Stepping underneath the waterfall shower head, I rubbed her shoulders in what was intended to be a comforting manner. She pulled away from me.

"I'm fine, Zo. Let's just get ready so we can go."

"Okay."

We washed our bodies and finished getting dressed in silence. I was sitting on the edge of the bed stepping into my Prada loafers when Alana came out of the closet fully dressed.

"Is this okay?"

I looked over Alana's appearance. She wore her hair straight down her back with a center part and had on minimal makeup. She dressed in a simple but form-fitting knee-length black turtle-neck dress. It was conservative enough for the occasion. It was hard to conceal her curves.

"You look nice," I told her.

I got up from the bed and walked towards her before kissing her on the cheek. Alana stepped away from me to pick up a small clutch purse and her cell phone.

"I'll be in the car," she said walking out of the room.

The days since PO's murder were tough for everyone in our crew, especially Alana. She wasn't a naturally emotional person, and she wasn't the best at expressing her feelings – especially feelings of sadness. However, I knew how significant this loss was for her. Without any living blood relatives around, PO, Kiara, and their daughters had become Alana and Marcus's family. PO's murder was a painful reminder of her uncle's death. Even though she was not able to vocalize it, I knew that Alana was struggling. I was there for her as much as I could be, but there was also business that I needed to handle. Courtney and the boys were still gone for a few more days, so I was able to spend my free time with Alana. When I wasn't with her, I was in the streets taking care of the day to day business and trying to figure out who was responsible for PO's death.

I finished getting together and joined Alana in my truck. The funeral was a blur. The church was packed, and the emotion level was high. Kiara nearly fainted when they closed the casket, and the girls were inconsolable throughout the service. I had a front-row seat to it all since Kiara insisted that we sit with the family. I sat next to a stoic Alana, who allowed me to hold her hand but barely showed any emotion. At one point, a lone tear fell from her eye, but she quickly wiped it away. I knew Alana better than most people, but in this situation, I was unable to read her emotions. At the repast, we were a bit more separated. While she occupied PO's daughters, I spent a considerable amount of time speaking to various different business associates. I was wrapping up a conversation with JB when Lucas Malone, Aaron Mercer's right-hand man and the number two in charge for the Cartel, approached us.

"JB, what's good?" Luke asked as the two men greeted each other.

"Ain't shit, man. Just kinda fucked up about all of this," JB answered.

Luke nodded. "That's definitely understandable. It's a fucked-up situation," he said. After a slight pause he said, "Let me speak to Zo real quick. I'll get up with you before I leave."

JB nodded and walked off. Luke turned toward me.

"How you holding up, man?"

I shrugged my shoulders. "Okay I guess ... all things considered."

"Yeah I feel you. This shit is so crazy. PO had just gotten everything back on track. Atlanta had finally gotten straight."

"Yeah, I know."

"Unfortunately, Aaron couldn't make it, but I'm here on his behalf to pay our respects," Luke stated.

"I appreciate it."

Luke nodded in acknowledgement. "I'm also in town to talk business. There are some things we need to discuss. I know today might not be the best time. I'm in town for another day or two so let me know what works best."

"I think I'll be occupied the rest of the day, but I'll definitely get at you tomorrow."

I saw Alana approaching from the corner of my eye.

"Excuse me," she said quietly.

Luke stepped back to give us a little space.

"I'm ready to head home."

"Right now? I'm kind of in the middle of something, but if you can give me a few minutes –"

Alana shook her head and waved me off. "I'm gonna catch a ride home with Yanni. I'm on her way."

I frowned. "La ... you sure?"

"Yeah. I'll talk to you later."

"I'll come by the house tonight."

She shrugged her shoulders. "Okay."

Alana kissed me on the cheek and walked off, leaving me confused by her demeanor. I shook my head and walked over to Luke shrugging my shoulders.

"Well, looks like my afternoon just cleared up. I can be free in about an hour or so if you want to have that conversation today," I told him.

"Bet. I'll meet you at your place."

❧ 4 ❧
ALANA

Megan Woods was never what you would consider a decent mother. To be completely honest, I can't remember a time that I ever viewed her as an actual maternal figure. She had my brother, Marcus, when she was young – around fifteen years old. Never really excited about school to begin with, she dropped out of high school the same year. Marcus's father didn't claim or take any responsibility for him. With a weak educational background, no help from her partner, and little to no support from her own mother, Megan got by however she saw fit. She accumulated a criminal record for things like petty theft and shoplifting. Four years later, I was born as a result of a one-night stand with some guy my mother met at a neighborhood house party.

Although we shared the same mother, Marcus and I looked nothing alike. My brother had a caramel skin complexion and was significantly taller than me – standing at five foot eleven. He always had a muscular physique, but as we grew older, he had developed a build that rivaled many amateur bodybuilders. He had a handsome although sometimes menacing face with piercing hazel eyes. Everything about my appearance was the complete opposite of his. I was shorter, darker, and although I had always tried to control my weight, I was thick by nature.

After I was born our mother's financial struggles worsened. I was told that my father tried to stick around and help Megan out, but he couldn't have stayed around for too long. I certainly don't remember him. Regardless of how long he did or did not stay, Megan's money problems continued. She had more and more trouble providing for my brother and me. Because of that, my brother and I spent more and more time bouncing between the homes of family members and friends.

When things got really bad, Megan turned to drugs. That made life even harder for us. Our mother picked one no good boyfriend after another. The men in her life changed often and were based on which one supplied her with the most money or drugs. I was in elementary school. I should have been learning grammar and multiplication facts instead of learning the difference between crack and cocaine. When I should have been playing outside and watching cartoons, I was learning the difference between semi-automatic and automatic weapons. That made for interesting cafeteria talk in the third grade. Marcus and I both started acting out at school. It felt like we were suspended more often than we were actually present. One school year Marcus was one suspension away from being sent to alternative school.

I spent most of my time at my best friend Porsha's house because I didn't want to go home and see my mother under the influence and whatever man she was entertaining that week. Sometimes Marcus and I went to school hungry in the morning and came home even hungrier in the afternoon because Megan used our lunch money for her next fix. A few of our family members tried to step in and help, but there was only so much they could do when Megan was constantly pushing them away and telling them to mind their own business.

By the time I reached the fifth grade, things were spiraling downhill fast. One time Megan left the house high on a Tuesday, and we did not see her again until she returned home on Friday ... high again. I had no respect for her. We fought constantly. I didn't call her mom, mommy, none of that. She was just Megan to me. Sure, she had given birth twice, but she was nobody's mother – just another woman. I resented her more and more each day. Hell, she resented herself, and it started showing with her failing health. She died of drug-related heart failure when I was eleven years old.

I hated to think in such a way, but I thought that things would have gotten better with my mother gone. In a way they did get a little better, but it still wasn't an ideal home life situation. After Megan died, Marcus and I moved in with our uncle – Megan's younger brother Darrell. He was one of the few family members that continuously attempted to help Megan while she was alive. We had a roof over our head, clean clothes, and three meals a day. He took better care of us than our mother ever had.

But by the time I reached middle school, I was well aware of how Uncle Darrell made his money. Uncle Darrell was best friends with PO and worked with him for years. At first, I was conflicted that my uncle worked with the very thing that ruined Megan's life. However, I quickly learned that money didn't grow on trees, and Megan ruined her own life with her poor decisions. Uncle Darrell did what he had to do to take care of himself and us. Soon his lifestyle began to appeal to Marcus and me. Although he wasn't initially excited about our desire to work alongside him, Uncle Darrell eventually went out on a limb to get us started with Julian Reid's organization under the umbrella of the Ramirez Cartel. When we got on and started making money, Nick and Zo wanted to get in too.

At first, our involvement was small time. Between the four of us, we took care of business on various corners, running packages, and any other necessary errands for the cause of the organization. I assisted in whatever way PO, Uncle Darrell, and Marcus allowed. Uncle Darrell didn't want me getting too involved because I was a girl. Marcus didn't want me getting my hands too dirty because I was his little sister. However, everybody could agree that in certain circumstances, I was the proper asset. Not too many cops in our neighborhood would suspect me of being involved in some of the things I was doing simply because of my looks. My physical appearance was both a gift and a curse as far as the streets were concerned. On one hand, I was able to get away with a lot because I wasn't under the same scrutiny as the guys. On the other hand, most people discredited me at first glance. Zo, Nick, and Marcus were all taller, intimidating males. I was a shorter than average attractive female. I literally had to fight to prove myself.

Then there were the guns. Everyone knew that I was hard-headed. Once I set my mind to something, there is almost no convincing me otherwise. Even though the guys preferred that I steered clear of their business, I kept my hands deep in it. They both decided that if I was determined to be in the streets that I needed to be able to take care of myself.

And I did.

Over time, things naturally progressed for our crew, and I was able to hold my own. Zo and Marcus went from being corner boys to climbing the ranks to some real power. Nick was content being a dealer. All was well until Uncle Darrell was murdered shortly after my eighteenth birthday. It was a trauma-tizing experience for me that changed my outlook on a lot of different things. One being my chosen career path. I no longer had the desire to work in the streets alongside my guys. Pleased with my change of heart, Marcus happily paid to send me to cosmetology school.

We all grew close with PO and his family over the years, but after Uncle Darrell died, I really felt like it was just Marcus and me. He was my first best friend. He would go to hell and back for me. Without Megan, Uncle Darrell or any of our other close relatives, Marcus and I leaned on each other. It was hard for me to adjust to being without him when he went to prison. I was ready for him to come home. I was informed that he was eligible for early parole and working through the process. My hopes were up as I prayed for good news.

So, when I saw Marcus's attorney calling my phone as I walked back into my house from PO's funeral, I answered quickly.

"Hey, Phil. What's going on?"

"Alana, I have some news for you," Marcus's attorney Philip Latimore stated.

His tone was jovial.

"Good news I hope."

"Excellent news," he said. "Your brother was granted parole and will be released early."

Excellent news indeed. I was grinning from ear to ear.

"You're right, Phil. Best news I've received in some time," I said. I stepped out of my heels and sat down on the couch in the family room. "I really needed some good news too."

Phil sighed. "Yeah. I'm sorry to hear about PO. I know how close you all were. Marcus was pretty upset when I spoke to him about it."

"Thanks, Phil. It's been a tough loss."

"Well, I don't want to hold you. Just wanted to share the good news. He should be out by early next week, but one of us will reach out to you with more details. I'm sure you or Zo are going to want to pick him up."

"Definitely. I look forward to hearing more soon."

We said our goodbyes, and I hung up the phone feeling happier than I had in a while. It had been a long three years without my partner in crime. When he was first locked up, I expected that he would be serving every day of his sentence. Marcus had never been good at following rules. Somehow, he had managed to keep his head down and stay out of trouble so that he was in a position to be paroled out early. I picked my phone back up to share the good news with Zo but hesitated before sending the text.

A lot had happened in the three years that Marcus had been

away. One being my relationship with his best friend. Zo and I debated back and forth about when and how to tell Marcus about our involvement, but we never actually got around to informing him. If Marcus was coming home as soon as I hoped, Zo and I needed to figure out something fast.

ZO

"So, what have you heard?" Luke asked.

I shook my head and took a sip from my glass of whisky. "Not much and that shit's stressing me," I answered.

After leaving the repast, Luke stopped by my place so we could talk in private.

"That's crazy man. Somebody has to know something," Luke said, sipping his own drink.

"I know, but I haven't come across any useful information," I said. "JB and a few other guys are on it. It's only been a couple of days. I'm sure something is going to come up soon."

"It needs to," Luke said. "Aaron's concerned about what PO's murder could mean for the state of things in Atlanta. We don't want a lot of confusion. Now that Aaron's taken over for his dad there's so much more he has to focus on here in the states and abroad. Besides ... you already know neither one of us like being up here."

We both shared a laugh because it was true. Both Luke and Aaron had been born and raised in Miami and were Florida boys at heart. They hated the unpredictable Georgia weather, especially during the winter. As we were rapidly approaching the cold weather months, I knew neither of them wanted to make an extended trip to Atlanta to fix things that had gone off course. The last time they came to Atlanta, they ended up spending way more time in the city then either of them wanted to. I knew what Luke stated about Aaron was true. He had an entire international operation to be concerned about – not just the happenings in one of his markets – regardless of how profitable Atlanta was.

"All bullshit aside ... you especially should want to get to the bottom of this," Luke said.

I nodded. "I know ... and I do. PO was like a second father to me. I can't just let this shit ride."

"Yeah, but *you* should especially want to know the reason behind his murder," Luke said, "especially if the motive was not personal and more about PO's position instead."

My face wrinkled in confusion as I sipped my drink.

"Because his position is now yours," Luke stated evenly. "Atlanta is yours, man."

I lowered my glass and gave Luke a sideways glance. "You for real?"

Luke nodded. "Dead serious," he said, sitting up straighter. "Come on man. You shouldn't be too surprised. PO was grooming you all along. Even when Aaron and I had to be here a couple of years ago, you always held shit down. By all accounts, you're the best man for the job. Why would we hand it to anyone else?"

I shook my head. "I don't know man," I said. "All this shit ... it's just a lot, man. Shit doesn't even feel real right now."

"You need to make it feel real, bruh. I definitely understand that you all are grieving right now, but the business doesn't stop. We gotta keep it moving for everyone's sake," Luke said. "Aaron wants you to get settled in your role as quickly as possible. We don't have time for a long transitional period. There doesn't need to be any uncertainty. Niggas need to know that we're not weak, and they need to know who is in charge."

"I feel you."

"So, we're going to move pretty quickly to get everything turned over to you," Luke said, "even the businesses in PO's name so money can continue to be cleaned seamlessly."

"What about Kiara and the girls?"

"I spoke with Tony, Julian's son in law. He handled a lot of

PO's personal legal affairs. There are life insurance policies and plenty of money left for Kiara. When we transfer all of the businesses into your name, we'll give her a substantial payout. Money will be the least of her troubles right now, but anything on top of that is up to you."

I nodded. "Well shit ... sounds like everything is pretty much planned out."

"Yeah man. You ready?" Luke asked.

"Hell yeah."

"Good," Luke said. He downed the rest of his drink. "I'll be here through tomorrow so let me know if you need anything else. Otherwise, Tony's going to reach out to you to handle all of the official paperwork necessary for business purposes. I'll be back next week once we get on the mayor's calendar for a sit down."

"Bet."

Luke stood up, and I joined him. He extended his hand, which I shook.

"Sorry again for your loss, man. PO was a real loyal, real special dude. He's going to be missed for sure," he said, "but at the same time, I have to wish you congratulations. I know you didn't want to get it like this, but you definitely deserve it, Zo. I'm excited to see what you're going to do with the team. Hopefully, in due time, you can find some way to enjoy and celebrate this."

"I appreciate it, Luke."

I walked him to the door. Luke stepped onto the porch and then turned around to face me.

"Zo, make sure your guys come up with something. We'll all breathe a little easier once we know who is responsible for this."

"We're on it."

Luke headed to his vehicle and left. After closing the door, I thought about calling Alana but stopped. Her mood had been off for days. Since I planned to see her later, I waited to talk to her until we were face to face. Instead, I headed to my room and changed out of the clothes I wore to the funeral. I left the house and met up with Nick and JB. After spending some time with them and recapping my conversation with Luke, I spent a few hours riding around solo checking on different areas of the business.

It was close to midnight when I pulled into the driveway of Alana's house. I used my key to let myself in and walked from room to room until I found her under the covers in her bedroom. The lights were off, and her back was facing me. Unsure if she was awake or not, I kicked off my shoes and stripped down to my underwear before climbing in the bed next to her. I moved close behind her, wrapping an arm around her waist. She started to stir when I kissed her shoulder.

"Hey," she said quietly.

"Hey."

"I've got something to tell you," she said with a yawn.

"Oh yeah? Me too."

Alana turned to face me. "Really? You go first."

I sighed. "I got up with Luke after we left the funeral. He and Aaron want me to take over for PO."

"What?" Alana asked. "That's major."

"I know."

"Wow, babe. This shit is so crazy," she said. "How are you feeling? Are you ready for this?"

I nodded. "Yeah. I am. PO and Julian made sure of it. It's crazy to think that neither one of them are here right now."

Alana sighed and rubbed the side of my face. "I know, baby. I know. I can't believe we lost them both in a matter of months. Shit doesn't even feel right," she said, "but I'm happy for you. Proud of you. I know you're going to hold it down. You were always better at this than the rest of us. You deserve this."

I kissed Alana on the lips. She always had a way of making me feel at ease. That was one of the qualities that made it hard for me to leave her alone in the beginning. The peace I felt with her was one of the reasons I kept pursuing a relationship with her even though I had a wife and kids at home. As we continued to kiss, I moved my hand from her waist to her thigh, rubbing it before I slid my hand up to her underwear. Alana giggled and pulled her lips from mine.

"Babe, I'm tired ... it's late ... and I already gave you some this morning," she laughed. "I told Ayanna I would open the shop in the morning."

I rolled onto my back, resting my head on the pillow and laughed as well. "I know. I was just trying my luck. We both could use some sleep," I sighed. "It was a long ass day."

"Yeah. It was."

I stared at the ceiling for a brief moment before closing my eyes. "What did you have to tell me though?"

I felt her shift in the bed while she hesitated to answer. I opened my eyes and turned to look at her.

"What's up, La?"

"Marcus is getting out next week."

"What?" I asked. "That's good news."

"Yeah. It is."

Alana's tone of voice lacked any sort of excitement. I looked at her expectantly.

"Why don't you sound excited?"

Alana sighed and caressed my chest. "Zo ... we have to tell him."

I let out a deep breath and pinched the bridge of her nose. She was right. We avoided sharing our relationship with Marcus for years. There were plenty of opportunities to tell him the truth. We often visited him together. We had several reasons why we chose to keep the information from him, but now we had no choice but to admit the truth. I had no idea how he was going to react, but I knew it wouldn't be good.

I turned to look at Alana in the darkness.

"Eventually," I said.

"Eventually?" Alana questioned with a frown. "What do you mean eventually? Zo, it's been three years. It was easy to keep it from him when he was behind bars, but I can't lie to my brother every day. He's going to be staying in this house for a while."

"I'm not asking you to lie –"

"It sounds like you are."

I paused and let out a frustrated sigh. "Look La, he ain't gonna be happy with either one of us when he finds out," I said. "Let's at least let him get situated and into the flow of things. Let me at least try to get the paperwork started with Courtney."

Alana turned on her side with her back facing me again. "Whatever, Zo."

"Babe ..."

"I said 'whatever'. I'll just keep lying to make things easier for you," she said. "Give you time to handle things with Courtney, right? Keep acting like I'm some sort of secret."

"You're not a secret," I said, touching her waist again.

"It sure feels that way."

Alana moved away from me and pulled the covers up to her shoulders. I rolled onto my back again and shook my head while staring at the ceiling. It had been a long day, and there was too much on my mind. I just wanted to go to sleep.

❧ 5 ❧
NICK

I looked at my watch to check the time. I spent the morning on a fact-finding mission with JB that was unsuccessful up until this point. I leaned across the hood of JB's Mustang and watched while he spoke with Shooter, a former dealer for Prime, while we were in the parking lot of a grocery store. Prime had been in charge of the trap that I took over. From what Zo said, he initially showed promise and high profits, but he was a consistent fuck up that tested the limits one too many times. He eventually took it too far. PO ended up getting rid of him, which set the stage for me to take charge. I brought my own crew along with me and effectively made all of Prime's former crew unemployed unless they were able to get on with someone else. From my understanding, Shooter was still out of work.

"Look man, I shouldn't even be talking to you for real," Shooter said to JB, while cutting his eyes at me, "and why does your man have to be here? I don't even know dude like that."

I smirked and shook my head.

"Yo, you got a problem?" Shooter asked me.

"JB, get your dog on a leash," I responded. "I ain't in the mood, and I promise he don't want this smoke."

Shooter cocked his head to the side and moved as if he was

43

going to come around to my side of the car. JB gently pushed Shooter in the chest, slightly sending him backwards.

"Chill," JB said evenly.

"Man, what the fuck is your problem?" Shooter asked me.

I stood up straight and shoved my hands into my pockets. "Ain't no problem unless you make one, Chief. Now look, you told my man here you had some info ... get that shit out so we can get the hell on. I ain't got all day to be out here with y'all."

Shooter looked to JB to see if he was going to address me. He didn't. I didn't have to be a boss to have similar respect. JB and I had been friends for years, but just being Zo's brother held a certain amount of weight in the streets. Anybody with any sense knew better than to try me. Shooter shook his head and finally started to get to the point.

"Look man ... it ain't a secret that PO got rid of Prime. Word on the street is that your new boss was there too," Shooter said. "I know he rubbed people wrong and messed up a couple of times, but Prime was bringing in major cash and putting his people on. Some people feel like it was kinda foul how PO did him. Niggas ain't too happy about that shit."

"Niggas like who? You?" I asked. "If memory serves me correctly, you got put out of business when Prime died too."

Shooter shot me a hard look and turned towards JB, who was also waiting for an answer. Shooter released a frustrated sigh and shook his head.

"Nah man. I ain't have nothing to do with it," he said. "If I was involved, why the fuck would I be here telling you this shit?"

I shrugged my shoulders. "You're asking me to get inside the mind of a snitch. Nigga, I don't know."

Shooter's face twisted into a frown. "You know what –"

"Just get to the point, man," JB said forcefully. "Who are the niggas that you're talking about? You gotta give me something worth my time, man."

"It wasn't none of us that had been down with Prime since jump. It was them new niggas from New York," Shooter explained. "They were trying to get their foot in the door down here. Apparently, they had tried to get in with Julian before he retired, but he and PO shut it down. So, they reached out to Prime because they know one of his cousins. They saw an opportunity because he was making so much money. Prime put them on for a little bit. They were making good money too, but when PO killed Prime that shut the door on them again. That shut down their opportunity to make some major cash and create a name for themselves down here. They were kind of hot about that shit."

"Hot enough to take PO out?" JB asked suspiciously. "I don't know if that sounds right."

"That's what I heard, man. A lot of the old crew is still in contact with them," Shooter stated. "I ain't lying man. You can ask Lil Chris or any of them. They'll tell you the same thing."

"So why didn't Lil Chris or anyone else reach out when Zo put a bounty on them niggas heads?" JB asked. "If everybody supposedly knew, why are you the only one talking?"

"Because they not trying to help y'all out. Your man over there put them out of work too."

"So why are you here?" I asked. "You ain't been working either. The same thing you're saying I did to them is exactly what I did to you."

"Because I need the money," Shooter answered quickly. "My Grandma's sick, and my girl is pregnant. I need some cash man. It don't matter how I get it."

I was skeptical as hell, but it was the only real lead we received since PO's death. Something about Shooter seemed shady to me. However, his sob story made things a little more believable. If the situation with his grandma and his girl was true, then he really did need money. Desperate niggas do desperate things. I knew better men than him that flipped on their crew when they were hard up for money. JB looked at me, and I nodded my head in approval.

"Alright man," JB said, turning back towards Shooter. He

reached in his pocket and pulled out a wad of cash. He peeled off a large number of bills and handed the money to Shooter. "That's half now. I need names and information on how to find these niggas. You'll get the other half when the job is done."

That was all I needed to hear. I hopped back in the passenger seat while JB wrapped up his conversation with Shooter. I texted my brother to let him know that we had found some promising information and that I would fill him in soon. A few moments later, JB hopped into the driver seat and took off.

"Where you trying to go?" he asked me.

"Back to the spot. I gotta meet up with Zo in a little bit," I answered. "We're going to pick up Marcus today."

"Oh word? My nigga Marc getting out today, huh?" JB asked.

I nodded.

"That's what's up," he said. After a moment or two, he changed the subject. "So, what you think about that shit Shooter was just talking?"

I shrugged my shoulders. "It's the most information we've received so far. Sounds like it could be true, but I suppose we'll find out in due time. I would stay on Shooter though. Zo is going to want that information ASAP."

"You know I'm on it," JB said.

I hoped JB's statement was true and that we would get to the bottom of everything quickly. Finding PO's killer was a directive from Aaron Mercer, and I understood why. The sooner we wrapped it up the sooner we could all relax and return to business as usual. The Atlanta operation had been through a lot in the last couple of years. Still, when PO took charge, he quickly restored things to the level of productivity and profitability that the Mercer family expected. We needed to keep our focus on keeping things moving in the right direction. Also, I didn't want to worry about someone being after the position itself and coming for my brother next.

. . .

Zo

The GPS told me we would be arriving at our destination soon. I sat in the passenger's seat of Nick's ride while he continued our drive. I checked my messages, confirming that Alana had not responded to me all day, and shook my head. There were many things I loved about her, but her attitude was not one of them. I exited the messaging app and sat my phone back in my lap. There wasn't any point in sending her another text when I knew I would be seeing her later.

"I don't know though, bruh. Something seems a little off about it," Nick continued to speak.

He was telling me about the meet up he and JB had earlier in the day with Shooter. It was the only useful information we received since PO's death. I definitely wanted to do some more digging. If Shooters information was correct, those guys were as good as gone as far as I was concerned.

"Why do you say that?"

Nick shrugged his shoulders. "I don't know. Shooter just seems shady as fuck. Nigga had shifty, beady little eyes and shit. I just don't know if I trust it."

I laughed loudly. "Beady little eyes and shit?" I continued to laugh. "Nick, what the fuck, man? He can't help the way his eyes look. He was born with that face."

"Nah, bro. You had to be there," Nick stated without laughter. I laughed even harder, because he was serious. "He couldn't maintain direct eye contact with either one of us. You know how I feel about niggas that can't look me straight in my eyes."

"Yeah I know, man," I laughed. "I know. We're going to get to the bottom of it. I don't want this shit hanging over my head, and I need to give Aaron and Luke some answers."

Nick nodded and navigated the vehicle onto the grounds at Riverbend Correctional Facility.

"Shit, I hope that Shooter's info checks out so we can be done with this shit," I said. "If it is true, I'mma have a job for Marcus sooner than he thought."

Marcus had always been a shoot first ask questions later type of guy. If I asked him to get rid of someone, he wouldn't even ask me why.

"Aye, you talked to Alana today?"

Nick gave me a confused look before cutting his eyes back in front of him and trying to find a place to park.

"Yeah," he answered. "I talked to her when I was out with JB. She's running a few errands for Marc after she leaves the shop, but she's gonna meet us at my place later."

I nodded. "Alright."

Nick cut his eyes at me again. "You haven't spoken to her?"

I shook my head. "But that's another conversation for another day. Let's just get our boy."

It had been a long three years since Marcus went to prison. He missed all the drama with KS9, the death of Deuce Reid and Caleb Bridges, the Reid's battle with the Pitt Twins, Julian's retirement, and both Julian and PO's deaths. I was excited to have one of my oldest, closest friends back in the streets with me. Especially with my newfound position, I wanted people around me that I knew I could trust.

I breathed a sigh of relief when he and Nick approached the car. I hopped out of the passenger seat eager to greet my friend.

"My boy," I said, as we bearhugged each other. "It's good to see you."

"Shit, it's good to be seen," Marcus said with a wide smile. "Where's my sister? I thought she would be with y'all."

Nick looked at me over Marcus's shoulder. I refused to make eye contact with him.

I shrugged my shoulders before I answered. "She's getting things ready for you. We'll meet up with her later."

"That's what's up," Marcus said. "I'm ready to get home."

"Then let's go."

We all hopped in the car, and Nick started the nearly two-hour drive from Milledgeville back to Atlanta. Along the way, we stopped to get Marcus some real food and then continued to

Nick's house. During the drive, we filled Marcus in on damn near everything – everything except for my relationship with his sister. We talked about the shooting, PO's death, and everything Shooter said. Marcus wasn't even back in Atlanta yet and was already down to help avenge PO's murder. I was just ready to have him back in the streets with me. He and Nick were my left and right hands. Now that we were all back together, I knew that we were going to be unstoppable. I felt confident that when it was all said and done, we would take the Atlanta organization to a level it had never seen before.

The gang was back together again, and I was focused. I had a 'to do' list a mile long, but there were a couple of bullet points at the top. First, I needed to help get Marcus situated. Then, I was going to handle my situation with Courtney for once and for all. I was tired of being in a loveless marriage. Courtney and I had not been on good terms for far too long. I knew that if she hadn't given birth to my boys that I would have been left. Alana deserved more from me than what she was getting. If Marcus was ever going to be okay with our relationship, I had to be a free man.

6

ALANA

"Damn girl. I had to find the tightest dress I could when you told me we were going out tonight," Porsha, said as she checked her makeup in her compact mirror. "It's been three long years since I laid eyes on that delicious looking brother of yours. He was big and fine before, but I bet he's prison big and fine now. I got to see it in person."

"Oh my God," I said, rolling my eyes and opening my car door. "I will never know what you see in him."

Porsha got out of my passenger's seat and started to walk with me towards the club's entrance. Knowing each other since we were six years old, Porsha was my oldest friend. She knew me better than most people, and she had been there for me through everything – the good and the bad. The heads of many men hanging out in the parking lot turned in our direction while we walked towards the club, our heels clicking against the pavement along the way. Porsha had always been an attractive girl, but like usual she was oblivious to the attention. Instead, she chose to keep talking to me about Marcus.

"Quit being such a hater. We're all grown. If your brother is interested, don't block me," she said. "Besides, you already have your man. Let me get mine."

"I don't have anything," I mumbled.

Porsha frowned. "What do you mean? What's up with Zo?"

I stopped walking. "I don't want to get into it right now," I said, "and try not to bring him up tonight, please."

Porsha's eyes widened.

"La! You haven't told your brother?"

I rolled my eyes with a heavy sigh. "Just keep your mouth closed about it, Porsha."

I started walking again, and Porsha jogged to catch up with me. "Of course," she said. "Your secret's safe with me. Always."

Porsha and I quickly made it inside the crowded, popular nightclub and went in search of our group of people. Marcus had been home for a couple of days, and we had gotten some friends together to celebrate his homecoming and enjoy our Saturday night. I spotted our crew in VIP. They had a whole section and a ton of bottles. It appeared that the fun had started without us. I greeted some of the guys along the way to reaching my brother, who was seated between Nick and Zo. I hugged his neck.

"Sis, what's good?" Marcus asked, taking a sip from the cup in his hand. "I thought you would have been here by now."

I shrugged my shoulders. "I got ready at Porsha's house. You know it takes a minute to make this kind of magic happen," I answered, referencing our appearance.

"Hey Marcus," Porsha said with a wide smile.

Marcus lowered his cup and returned Porsha's smile. "Hey," he said. "I guess the delay was worth it. Y'all look nice tonight."

I was only a half-hour later than I said I would arrive, but I could tell Marcus was already drunk. He tapped Zo and pointed towards Porsha and me.

"Don't they look good?"

Zo shrugged his shoulders. "Yeah they look alright," he said before sipping his own drink.

I rolled my eyes at Zo's nonchalant response. We had barely seen each other, and our communication had been strained since the night of PO's funeral.

"Just alright?" Porsha laughed. "This dress costs me way too much money to just look alright."

"Don't mind him," Marcus said to Porsha. "That dress looks damn good on you. Matter of fact ... Nick, scoot down so Porsha can have a seat."

I laughed and shook my head at my best friend and brother. My eyes briefly met with Zo, who continued to glare at me while he sipped his drink. It was obvious that there was tension between us, but it wasn't the time or place for all of that. I broke my eye contact with him while Porsha sat down next to Marcus. Moving in the opposite direction of them, I walked over to an empty spot on the couch next to Nick's girlfriend, Kayla. I was in desperate need of a drink. I poured myself a cup and relaxed on the couch. A few of my other friends planned to stop by, and I was anxiously watching the door. With Porsha abandoning me to cozy up to my brother, I needed another distraction to help me avoid Zo for the rest of the night.

Luckily, a few of my friends showed up not too long after my arrival. After a few hours and several drinks, I was dancing and having a good time instead of worrying about the presence of my married boyfriend. I downed the last of my cup and excused myself to use the restroom. I quickly handled my business and freshened up before exiting the bathroom and stepping into the hallway. I let out a heavy sigh when I looked up to see Zo standing there as if he had been waiting for me.

I couldn't stop the frown from coming to my face.

"What do you want?"

"I want to know what your problem is," he answered, stepping closer to me.

"I don't have a problem," I quickly responded. "I'm fine."

"You're fine? Come on, Lala. You say that shit so often ...I know you don't even believe it."

I sighed and looked down at my feet, smoothing down the front of my dress before I looked back up at Zo.

"I don't want to do this tonight," I told him.

"If not now, then when? I've barely spoken to you all week. Since Marcus is staying with you, it's not like I can come by the house later."

"And I sure as hell can't come by yours," I snapped.

Zo released a frustrated sigh. "So, you're upset about Courtney? You're upset because I asked you to wait to tell your brother? What's the problem, La?"

"No, Lorenzo. It would be ridiculous for me to be upset about Courtney. I knew you were married when I let you into my bed three years ago."

"If that's not it, then what's the problem? I told you I was going to take care of it, and I am. Your brother and I have some important things to take care of with work in the upcoming weeks, but I promise ... as soon as that's taken care of –"

"Zo, I told you that's not it. We've been doing what we've been doing for a few years. What's a couple more weeks?"

I shook my head and tried to walk away. He grabbed my arm and pulled me back towards him.

"La, talk to me," he said. "Your whole mood has been off since PO died. Is this what your grief looks like?"

I let out a deep breath. I didn't want to do this at somebody's damn nightclub. I didn't want to have this conversation period, but there I was in the middle of my feelings when I should have been celebrating my brother and getting drunk with my girls.

"You know what I've been thinking about since PO died?" I asked.

"Enlighten me."

"Kiara," I said. Zo looked confused, so I continued. "All those years they were together without getting married, and what does she have to show for it? Three kids and some money he left behind? She's not getting the businesses, and she never had his last name. In the program, she was listed as his *loving companion.*"

"La, what does that have to do with you? With us?"

"I'm glad you weren't seriously hurt, but that was the second time you've been shot since we started ... whatever this is that we're doing. If you died tomorrow, what would happen to me? What would I have to show for the past few years? Nothing. Fuck being listed as a companion. I wouldn't be mentioned at all."

Zo shook his head and sighed. He placed his hands on my hips and tried to pull me towards him. I backed up.

"No, Zo. Don't," I said, pushing his hands away. "I knew what I was signing up for when we started fucking around. I shouldn't be bothered by it now."

Zo reached for me again. This time he wrapped his arms around me in a tight embrace I couldn't escape.

"Listen to me ... Courtney and I are done. I'm going to make that official as soon as I can," he said. "I know it's not fair for me to ask you to wait any longer, and I hate that you feel like a secret. You deserve much more than that, and I'm going to give it to you, La. I promise."

I allowed him to continue hugging me. Despite my frustration, I believed him. Our situation wasn't perfect, but he didn't have a habit of lying to me. If he said he was going to do something, I trusted that he was going to do it in his own time. He kissed me on my forehead.

"Really? Y'all gotta chill with all that shit."

I quickly pulled away from Zo, looking around to see Nick standing a few yards from us. He shook his head and walked closer. Zo dropped his arms, releasing me from his embrace.

"Come on, bruh. What if Marcus had to use the bathroom? How would you explain that?"

Zo shook his head. "You're right, man. You're right."

I shook my head and walked away from them. I had friends waiting and a whole bottle of brown liquor with my name on it. My drama with Zo could wait for another day.

MARCUS

I navigated the parking lot until I found a spot not too far away from the front door of Alana's salon. Since she had a new car, Alana was letting me use her Nissan Altima until I got my own ride. I had a little time to kill before I met up with my people, so I decided to visit my sister at work. I made my way into the salon, greeting people politely while being directed to her office. I knocked on the slightly cracked door before pushing it open. Alana smiled when she saw me and ended her phone call.

"Hey," she greeted me, sitting the desk phone back on the receiver. She got up for a hug. "Have a seat."

I sat down in one of the chairs at her desk while she returned to her seat. "This is a nice spot," I told her.

"Yeah. Ayanna and Jada really did a great job with this place. The location is perfect. We offer a wide variety of services, and with the range of stylists, estheticians and nail techs we have, we're really able to attract a large clientele."

"I don't know what all that means, but it sounds like you're making a ton of money," I laughed.

"Hell yeah," Alana laughed as well.

"Good deal," I said. "Nice to see your high maintenance ass can finally afford yourself."

Alana laughed at my joke. Even though she had completed cosmetology school, Alana was still working for Julian Reid when I got locked up. She had a hard time walking away from the fast money. Only when her career really took off did she decide it was time to leave the streets alone. I was concerned about her while I was locked up, so I asked Zo to look out for her while I was away. However, it appeared that she was doing a good job taking care of herself in my absence.

"Nice to see you though," Alana started, "since you haven't been home since the night before your party."

I shrugged my shoulders. "I've been out and about," I

answered with a smile. "I spent part of the weekend with your girl, Porsha."

Alana rolled her eyes.

"Oh, Lord."

I laughed and said, "But then I've really just been busy getting up to speed on business with Zo. I spent the other part of the weekend crashing with JB. It looks like I'm jumping right in the middle of some shit."

"Some shit like what?" Alana asked with a raised eyebrow.

I shook my head at her. "Come on, sis. You know that's not your life anymore. You don't need to know those types of details."

Alana shrugged her shoulders.

"You're right," she said with a smile. She waved her arms around. "This is my life now."

"Damn right," I said, "and it looks good on you. Nice ass car, nice ass house, and a job doing something you actually love ... Uncle Darrell would be proud."

Alana nodded with a smile on her face. She changed the subject and asked, "Are you free for lunch?"

"Nah. I just stopped by to see where you worked. Just a little pop up," I told her. "I gotta go meet up with the crew."

"Okay. You coming home tonight?"

I shrugged my shoulders and stood up. "I don't know. Probably not, but if anything changes, I'll let you know."

"Alright. Just let me know," she said, "and if you're going to be MIA for a few days just shoot me a text and let me know you're okay. You just got home. I'd like to know that you are safe and sound."

"Yes, ma'am," I laughed.

I understood her concern. We had lost a number of people close to us. I had a couple of jail stints here and there but never had to do any real time until my last arrest. She just got me back. She didn't want to lose me again.

"I'll text you later, sis."

I hugged and kissed my sister on the forehead before leaving her shop and heading back to my car. Before I could start the engine, I felt a vibration in my pocket. When I got released from prison, Alana provided me with a new cell phone. I had only been home for a week. Very few people had the number. I looked at the screen to see a text message from Zo asking me if I was on the way. I responded, letting him know that I was in route and would be there shortly.

What I didn't tell him was that I had another quick stop to make along the way.

I left my sister's salon and headed towards my destination. I pulled into the parking lot of a convenience store and drove over to a familiar Chevy sedan. I put the car into park, but I kept the engine running. It was going to be a quick stop. I unlocked my doors right as the person I was meeting approached my passenger door.

"What's up man?" Shooter said, sliding into the car.

"Ain't shit," I said. "Headed to go meet up with my people."

Shooter nervously looked around the parking lot.

"Fuck you looking around for?" I asked with a frown.

"I don't know, man," he said, shaking his head.

I shook my head at him with narrowed eyes. "You ain't gotta worry about shit. I ain't even gonna be here that long," I said. "Did you tell Zo's people what they wanted to hear?"

Shooter nodded. "Yeah, man. Everything we talked about, and they ate that shit up too. They bout to be on them New York niggas ass."

"Good. The sooner we get rid of them, the sooner we can all put this shit behind us."

"For sure."

I opened the center console and pulled out a rubber-banded stack of cash. Shooter's eyes lit up, and he quickly took the money from my hand. I fought the urge to shake my head. The nigga was money-hungry as hell. I was glad he was working alongside me for the time being, but I knew I couldn't trust him for long. I quickly discovered that he would do just about anything if he thought the payout was worth it in the end. A person like that could never be trusted to be loyal.

"Alright man. I'mma get up with you later," I told him, giving him the cue to exit my ride. "Looks like I'm about to be busy tracking down some niggas from New York."

"Bet. Let me know if you need anything else," Shooter said, exiting the car. "You know I got you."

I nodded but didn't verbally respond. I knew he hadn't told the complete truth. I only had him until the next man with deeper pockets came along.

7
ZO

ONE MONTH LATER

Mayor Richardson laughed at my lame ass joke so hard I thought he was about to spit out his water. I was getting real good at entertaining uppity ass negroes like him. That worked in my favor. We didn't have to be friends like he and Julian Reid once were. This was strictly business. I knew that as long as I stayed in his good graces that my team was practically untouchable in the eyes of law enforcement. That was all I cared about. My best friend had recently gotten home from a prison bid, and I wanted to make sure no one else close to me ended up behind bars.

"You know what," Mayor Richardson said, wiping the corners of his mouth with his cloth napkin. "I like you. You've got a lot of personality, man."

I smiled and shrugged my shoulders before taking a sip of my drink.

"I'm glad things are continuing to move along so well. It's a shame that we lost PO, but in such a short amount of time you have proven to be a worthy replacement. Aaron and Luke told me you were good, but I'm sure you can understand why I may have initially been hesitant," he said.

"Of course. I'm another new face. Another new person for you to conduct business with," I said. "Another person to put your trust in, but I think we both know that trust is the only way this is going to work."

"Exactly," the mayor said, pointing in my direction. "It seems that we have gotten off to a good start, and I only hope it continues from here."

"Me too."

I glanced at my watch. I finished my meal a while ago. I was just entertaining the mayor until I needed to head over to my lawyer's office. Over the last couple of weeks, my crew had been after Prime's New York associates, knocking them off one by one to avenge PO's murder. Our moves had been quiet and calculated so that we were able to handle our mission without alerting the mayor or police chief. There were only two men left to take care of – the leader of their crew, Tank, and his partner, Rome. We had spent the past week looking for them with no luck. I was starting to think they had cut their losses and went back up north. With that matter of business behind us and Marcus reacquainted with the team, I was sticking true to the words I told Alana. I was working with my attorney to get the ball rolling on my divorce from Courtney.

I did not expect our split to be amicable, but I was prepared to be more than fair. Courtney could keep the house, her cars, and I was willing to give her more than enough money to take care of herself and our boys. I just wanted to be done with our marriage. I wanted to be with the woman I really loved – the woman that I knew loved me. After I left my meeting with the lawyer, I planned to tell Alana in person that all the waiting, lying, and secrecy would be over soon. We were a week away from Thanksgiving, and I hoped to be a free man shortly after the start of the New Year.

"Lorenzo, it's been a pleasure doing business with you so far, and I surely hope it continues. Unfortunately, I have to get back to the office," he said, placing his napkin on his empty plate. We both stood up, and he reached to shake my hand. "I'll speak with you soon, but in the meantime let me know if you need anything – anything at all."

I nodded as I watched the mayor gather his things and head for the exit. After taking care of the bill, I headed for my truck. Before I could get behind the wheel, my phone started ringing.

"What's up?" I greeted my brother.

"Bro, we got a location on that boy Rome."

"Yeah?" I asked, checking my watch again. "Where about?"

I listened to my brother tell me where we could find one of our last remaining targets. I had to make a quick decision whether I was going to go to the meeting with my lawyer and risk losing Rome for good or reschedule for another day. I knew what I needed to do.

"Alright man. I'm leaving lunch with the mayor," I said, sliding behind the wheel of my truck. "I'm headed there now."

"Bet. I'm already in route with Marcus. What's the plan?"

I started my engine and began to tell my brother what I wanted to do while I drove to meet up with him. About twenty minutes later, I pulled onto the street where the older ranch style house Nick described was located. I passed Nick's empty car parked near the corner and stopped several yards ahead. Since Nick and Marcus were not in the car, I assumed they were already in position. I got out with my 9mm secured in my waist-band. Casually walking down the sidewalk, I sent a text to Nick telling him I was there. I continued towards the house, observing my surroundings along the way. It was surprisingly quiet outside with no other cars parked near the house in question. There was no garage to the house, and the only car in the driveway was the Camry the guys said belonged to Rome's girl. I continued on to the front door.

Without any hesitation, I knocked on the door twice. I waited a few moments and then knocked again. This time I heard footsteps as they approached the door. The lock turned, and a few seconds later the door cracked open.

"Hello," a young woman I assumed to be Rome's girlfriend greeted me.

"Hey, is Rome here?" I asked.

A look of confusion appeared on the woman's face. "Uh, not at the moment."

"Damn," I said, acting like I was surprised. "He just told me to meet him over here."

The woman hesitated before cracking the door open a little wider. "I can call him real quick to see when he'll be back," she said. "He didn't tell –"

She was interrupted by movement at the backdoor. Nick was picking the lock. Seconds later, we both heard the door open and footsteps while Nick and Marcus made their way into the house.

"What the hell?" she asked, turning to look behind her and momentarily taking her hands off the doorknob.

I used her distraction as my opportunity to easily enter the house. I pushed against the door, opening it completely and stepping inside. The woman's eyes widened in horror when she turned back around to face me. I closed and locked the front door. Marcus and Nick entered the living room from the kitchen where the back door was located. She looked back and forth between them and me.

"I don't have any money," she said, defensively raising her hands.

Marcus sucked his teeth. "Bitch, does it look like I need your money?"

I frowned at Marcus while Nick shook his head.

"Man, chill."

"Why are you here? I didn't do anything, and I don't know anything," she said defensively.

"Don't worry about that," Nick said in a calmer tone of voice. "Ain't nobody here for you. Where's your man at?"

"My man? I – I don't know what you talking about."

I sighed and shook my head, pulling the gun from my waistband. Marcus tossed me a silencer that I started to attach to the gun.

"You just said you would call that nigga a moment ago," I said. "So, call him."

She didn't move towards her phone.

"Call him and say what?"

I frowned. "I don't give a fuck. Just get him over here ... unless you want to be my problem."

She looked from me to Marcus and Nick, who also had their guns pulled out. She looked back over to me and shook her head before pulling her cell from her back pocket. I watched while she called Rome.

"Hey baby ... yeah ... I was wondering when you were going to be back by this way ... yeah, I'm hungry ... okay. Sounds good. See you soon."

She hung up the phone and looked at me expectantly.

"Now what?" she asked.

"Now we wait," I said, sitting down on the couch.

Marcus and Nick sat down, and I motioned for her to have a seat as well. She hesitated but took a seat on a leather recliner. We waited in silence with the television as background noise. Twenty minutes later, we heard the key turn in the lock of the front door while Rome made his way into the house with bags of takeout food.

"Yo! What the fuck?" he shouted.

He dropped the bags of food and grabbed a pistol from his waistband. Marcus and Nick immediately hopped up with their guns aimed at him. Rome kept his gun drawn, waving it back and forth between Marcus and Nick. He turned to look at his girlfriend.

"What the fuck did you do? What you got me walking into?"

Rome's girlfriend started crying and shrugging her shoulders. "I don't know. I'm sorry."

Nick slowly moved towards Rome and the front door. He

pulled Rome further into the house by his shirt and pushed the door closed. Shaking his head, Rome broke his eye contact with his girlfriend and looked around before focusing on me. His eyes widened with recognition.

"Zo? What the fuck, man? What's going on?"

"If you know who I am, then you know why I'm here," I said calmly. "We know what you and your crew did, and you know I can't let that shit go. You see what's already happened to the rest of your squad."

Rome shook his head. "That wasn't us! You got that shit twisted, man. Tank ... Me ... none of us had anything to do with PO! Y'all out here killing the wrong niggas for nothing."

I shook my head and looked at Rome with my disbelief written all over my face. "I have a hard time believing that one, Rome. Everything we've heard has pointed right back to you and Tank."

"And I don't know who told y'all that shit, because word on the street is it was one of your people behind the shit," Rome said.

Marcus pistol-whipped him, knocking him down to his knees. He dropped his gun, which Nick quickly picked up. Rome shook his head and wiped at the blood dripping from his mouth.

"I don't know what streets you speak of," I said, shaking my head. "Honestly, that shit doesn't even make any sense."

Rome sighed and shook his head while he looked up at me. "Don't have to make sense to be true," he spat.

I looked up at Marcus, who was looking at me and waiting for my approval. There really wasn't a need for any more talking. I nodded slightly in Marcus's direction to give my consent.

"Man, come on. For real this ain't have shit to do with us," Rome said. "Shooter knows what's up. He said it was one of y'all. Some nigga named –"

Marcus pulled the trigger sending one shot through his temple. Rome's girlfriend started to scream. Marcus turned his gun, which also had a silencer, towards her and pulled the trigger again shooting her in the chest twice.

I stood up from the couch and tucked my gun back into my waistband.

"Lock the doors on your way out. Wipe it down, collect the casings, and get rid of the guns. All of them," I instructed them. "Call JB if you need help."

"Bet," Marcus said as he started to move around the house doing the things that I asked.

Nick approached me. "Damn bro. I forgot you were meeting up with the attorney today," he said looking at his watch. "You still got time to make it?"

I shook my head.

"Nah, but I called on my way over here. We're going to meet first thing in the morning," I answered. "Get the ball rolling so I can get that shit over with."

"Have you told Lala?"

"Nope. I'm going to stop by her place tomorrow after I leave the attorney's office."

"That's what's up," Nick said with a smile. He shook his head and laughed. "Look at you finally handling your business."

I laughed. "Finally," I said. I sighed when I looked around the living room. "Looks like we still have a little more business to take care of though. Continue to keep an eye out and an ear to the streets. If Rome was still in town, maybe Tank is too."

"For sure. I'll get with JB too."

"Bet."

I exited the house and casually walked back to my truck as if nothing had ever happened. My mind was already on the next task.

8

MARCUS

"Marcus! The food is almost done!" Alana called from the kitchen.

I yawned and stretched my arms before sitting up in the bed. Alana had awakened me on her way down to the kitchen to let me know she was preparing breakfast before she got ready for work. It was a little before ten o'clock – earlier than I usually started moving. However, I had not been to my sister's place in days, and I decided to check in and spend some time with her. Although we had taken care of Rome the day before, the crew and I were still trying to find Tank so we could get rid of him too. Zo was hell-bent on getting rid of anyone who had anything to do with the people he held responsible for PO's death. I was ready to tie up any loose ends.

I swung my legs over the side of the bed and paused for a moment before hopping to my feet. I pulled on a T-shirt and a pair of sweatpants before stepping into my slides. I yawned and stretched again before heading down the stairs to the kitchen. Alana greeted me and started making small talk. I slid onto one of the stools at the kitchen island while she put the finishing touches on the food. I silently admired the stainless steel and granite details of her kitchen. Alana started to ramble about her work at Ayanna Reid's salon and how well it was going. She was really adjusting to her management role. I only half listened to her. Instead, I was thinking about how well she had taken care of herself in my absence. Since we were younger, I had always looked out for her. I had always been the one to take care of her. Now she had proven that she could stand on her own two feet and handle her own business. I was a proud big brother.

"Ayanna said that she and Tony might try for another baby, and she's thinking about cutting back on her responsibilities," Alana said while she grabbed two plates from a cabinet. "If all goes well over the next couple of months, she is planning to sell the shop to me."

"Sell the shop?" I asked. "I thought she and Jada owned it together."

Alana shook her head and filled our plates with eggs, pancakes and sausage patties. "No. Jada turned it over to Ayanna when she moved to Miami," she answered with a big smile. "Ayanna talked to Jada about it anyway, and she's cool with it."

"That's what's up, but ... where you gonna get the money for the purchase?"

Alana shrugged her shoulders. "I've got some cash at my disposal."

"Damn, La. That's what's up. I'm proud of you."

Alana smiled and sat our plates down. She grabbed two glasses of juice and utensils before sitting next to me.

"I'm going to be a whole business owner. Who would have thought?"

Alana laughed to herself and took a sip of her juice. I had a mouth full of eggs when I heard the sound of a key turning in the lock on the front door. I turned to Alana with a questioning look only to be met with a look of alarm in her eyes. The door opened and closed, and the alarm was disabled before I heard footsteps headed in our direction.

"Babe! Where you at?"

The questioning look dropped from my face and was

replaced with a frown because I recognized the voice. I knew who had entered her home. I just had no idea why he had a key to my sister's house and why the fuck he was calling her 'babe'. Alana broke her eye contact with me and turned towards the arched opening to the kitchen right as Zo became visible.

"Hi," she greeted him.

"Hey ..." Zo's voice trailed off. He broke his eye contact with Alana to turn and look at me. "Marcus, what's up?"

I dropped my fork and stood up from the stool. "What's up? Nigga, you tell me what the fuck is up."

Zo sighed and shook his head. "Look man ... I know what you're probably thinking. It ain't even like that."

My face twisted into an angry frown, and I started towards my friend. Alana grabbed my arm.

"Marcus, don't."

I turned my scowl on my sister and shrugged her off before turning back to Zo.

"Fuck you mean it ain't like that? You came up in here with the pet names and shit ... and why the fuck do you have a key to her crib?"

I watched as Zo and Alana exchanged uneasy looks. Zo sighed heavily, and Alana shrugged her shoulders.

"Because he bought this house."

Alana's voice was quiet – timid even. She looked down at the hardwood floor in front of her instead of looking into my face. I was heated. Alana was making more than enough money on her own. In my mind, there was only one reason Zo would have purchased a house for her. I looked back at Zo, who maintained eye contact with me. I could feel my jaw twitching. When I was on my way to prison, I asked him – my best friend – to look after my sister. There was obviously something going on between them that I was unaware of – something they had tried to hide. Something they knew I would never approve. They both visited me several times while I was locked up. Neither one of them ever mentioned this shit. I never had a clue.

"Bruh ... bruh! You fucking my sister?"

Zo shrugged his shoulders. "It's more than that, Marc. This ain't a casual situation. I admit we probably should have told you sooner, but –"

"Ain't no fucking 'but' ..." I cut him off, waving my hands in front of me. "There shouldn't have been anything for you to tell me because whatever this is shouldn't have happened. I asked you to look out for her ... not fuck her behind my back!"

"And I'm telling you that it's deeper than that." Zo's voice was elevated and firm. "I love her."

"Love her?" I laughed, shaking my head in disbelief. "Nigga, you're playing with her! You got a wife and kids at home. How the fuck could you be serious about this?"

Zo shrugged his shoulders again. "Marc, you knew me and Courtney weren't right when you went away. That's a temporary situation that I'm taking care of."

"Temporary situation? You've been married to the bitch for seven years. Nigga, you out your goddamn mind."

I lunged at Zo, swinging my right fist at his head.

"Marcus, stop!" I heard Alana yell at me.

Zo ducked and pushed me in the chest, forcing me backwards. I stumbled but stayed on my feet.

"Chill, man. Damn!" Zo shouted.

I didn't stop, and I didn't chill. I charged at him again – this time I made contact by shoving him to the ground. There was no more talking on either of our parts. I was so mad I was seeing red. Zo had a few inches on me, but I had a few pounds on him. It was a fair fight in my eyes. As we continued to wrestle and throw punches, I could hear Alana yelling at us, but I had no idea what she was saying. I felt her hands pulling at my arm. I freed myself from her grasp and shoved her away, accidentally knocking her to the floor. On her way down, she hit her head on the glass kitchen table and then on the floor. Bumping into the table hard, she knocked over her glass candle holders and center-piece. The broken pieces of glass spread across the floor distracting me long enough for Zo to grab me by my shirt and slam my back against the floor.

"Calm down, bruh!"

Zo held on to my shirt tightly while he continued to keep me pinned down on the ground. I struggled against him, but he slammed me down again. He leaned into me with his full weight, keeping me in place. Zo looked over at my sister who sat up, rubbing the spot on her head that made contact with the table and the floor.

"You okay?" he asked her.

Alana glared at me with a frown on her face. "This shit hurt, but I'm fine." She got up and walked over to me. "Marcus, what the fuck?"

I didn't answer her. I stared at Zo.

"You gonna let me up?" I asked.

"You gonna chill?" he asked.

"Nigga, get the fuck off me!" I pushed against him again.

Zo shook his head and let me go. We both stood up, still glaring at each other. I turned towards Alana.

I shook my head at my sister and fixed my angry glare on her. "I can't believe he would do some shit like this, but Lala ... I'm so disappointed in you. I expected much more from you than being some married nigga's side chick. My best friend at that, La. This is some bullshit."

Alana didn't respond. Zo didn't say anything either. I shook my head at the both of them.

"Fuck this shit. I'm out ... and you ain't gotta worry about me staying here anymore either," I said. "I'll come back for my shit when I find somewhere else to stay."

"Are you serious right now?" Alana asked.

I ignored her and walked into the family room, grabbing my jacket and the keys to the Altima. Alana followed me.

"Marcus!"

I headed towards the front door. Without even looking at my sister, I opened and closed the door on the way out of the house

Zo had purchased for her. From the other side, I heard her call my name one last time.

"Marcus!"

NICK

"Then he had the nerve to say he didn't have anything to do with it," Marcus laughed while he told a few of the guys in the crew about our encounter with Rome.

I watched him out of the corner of my eye and fought the urge to shake my head at him. It was no secret that we were after Prime's former associates from New York. However, everyone didn't need to be in the loop about the how and when. Since taking over for PO, Zo kept a lot of things close, choosing to only let a few people in on the details concerning certain aspects of the business. His philosophy was that everything wasn't meant for everyone to know. Zo had always been smart in how he handled his business – smooth even. He had a business and logistical mind similar to Julian Reid, and he was also ruthless enough to handle the grimier side of the operation that took place behind the scenes. He liked nice things and the lifestyle that he was able to afford, but he wasn't flashy. He had never liked drawing unnecessary attention to himself.

Watching Marcus boast and brag about taking the lives of Rome and his girlfriend, I started to realize that he and Zo were polar opposites.

When we were younger, it was funny. It didn't bother me that Marcus was so loud and arrogant. However, we weren't kids anymore. At this stage in the game, we had so much more at stake. He should have known that more than anybody. He had been out of prison for less than two months. More than anyone, he should have wanted to lay low for a while. Instead, he was doing anything but maintaining a low profile. Since he got home, he was constantly trying to be the center of attention and making sure he was the loudest one in the room. It irritated me.

Zo always seemed to have blinders on when it came to Marcus. I knew if he were able to look at things objectively, he would be bothered by Marcus's behavior as well.

"If they didn't do it, then who did?" one of the guys asked shaking his head.

"Exactly. We ain't heard or seen nothing that points to anyone else," Marcus said. "But check this though, he had the nerve to say that he heard it was one of us. Talking about Prime's guy Shooter would know all the details. We don't even mess with Shooter. Why would he know anything about us? That's their man."

Several guys around the room frowned and shook their heads.

"Right. Why in the world would any of us have anything to do with taking out PO?" one of them asked.

"That's what I'm saying. That doesn't even sound right," Marcus said. "None of us gained anything from PO's death except Zo and –"

"Nah, bruh. Watch your mouth," I said from the corner of the room.

Marcus looked at me with narrowed eyes. "What I was about to say was that we all know Zo would have never made a move against PO. They were too close for that."

"I don't care what you were about to say. Ain't no point in even mentioning bruh," I stated firmly. "It's disrespectful to even say his name period in connection to some shit like that."

The room fell quiet while eyes darted back and forth between Marcus and me. It was the end of the week, and many of us were coming to drop off money before picking up product for the next week. The tension had risen quickly, but everyone in the room felt it.

"Alright man," Marcus said waving me off dismissively.

My face twisted in a frown. Marcus had always been an insti-gating troublemaker, but I wasn't a punk. The only person who was allowed to even remotely speak to me in a disrespectful tone was my brother. I dropped the duffle bags in my hands and started towards Marcus. JB grabbed my arm, holding me in place.

"He don't mean nothing by it," JB said low enough for only me to hear. "Just let it go and handle the business you came here for. We got enough going on as it is. We don't need no shit between y'all."

I hesitated before responding. I was still pissed, but JB was right. I could clear the air with Marcus another time when there wasn't an audience. Zo had taken a rare night off, and he would not be happy to hear about me popping off on Marcus in his absence. Especially without Zo there to witness the exchange, it would automatically be assumed that I was in the wrong. I decided to let it go for the time being.

Following JB's advice, I handled my business. After exchanging money and product, I got back in my ride with one of my dealers and headed back to the trap. I left him at the house with a few other guys to handle their work and got back in my ride. I dialed my brother's phone before I could pull away from the curb.

"What's up, Nick?" he answered.

"What are you up to?"

Wherever he was had a considerable amount of background noise.

"Daddy duties," Zo answered. "I took the boys to an arcade. What's going on?"

"You need to check your boy."

I heard Zo sigh heavily on his end of the line.

"What did you and Marcus get into it about this time? You know he's still mad about Alana and me."

"I understand that, but that doesn't have anything to do with business. You just need to make sure he's watching his mouth. I went to drop off my split, and he was in there talking about Rome."

"Oh yeah?" Zo asked.

I heard him pull the phone away from his mouth to say something to one of my nephews. I didn't have his full attention. Our conversation could wait, but eventually, we needed to talk about Marcus in detail. Hopefully we could have that conversation before Marcus became a problem.

"What was he saying?" Zo asked after a few moments.

I sighed. "We can talk about it later."

"You sure? I know it's loud over here, but we're actually about to leave in a minute."

"Yeah, bruh. It's cool. I know you were trying to spend family time," I said. "Let's just get up tomorrow."

"Bet. I'll talk to you then."

I ended the call shaking my head while I headed towards my next destination. Zo had always been closer to Marcus than I was. I was able to see Marcus for what he was — what he had become. He was displaying too many characteristics similar to Cameron Reid, and that wouldn't be good for any of us.

9

ALANA

"La ... are you there?"

Zo's voice came through the speakers of my car from the Bluetooth connection to my phone.

"Yeah ... I'm here."

"You ain't said nothing, baby. Talk to me."

I continued to steer my car, but I was on autopilot – not necessarily as focused on the road ahead of me as I should have been.

"I ... wow ... I mean, I'm happy, but I'm anxious to see how all of this is going to play out," I answered. "You're actually working on your divorce petition. I know we've talked about this for a while. It just doesn't feel real right now. If I feel like this, I can't even begin to think how Courtney is going to react to all of this."

"You don't have to worry about that. I'll deal with the fallout from her," he said. "I should have left a long time ago."

"She's going to know that we were involved before the divorce. She's not stupid. She'll put two and two together and –"

"Why does that matter?" Zo asked.

"If we're really going to be together, it matters. She's not going to be happy about me being around your sons."

"She's not going to keep me away from my kids. I can promise you that."

"Okay," I said releasing a deep breath.

I felt guilty. Of course, I knew that I had no business being involved with a married man from the beginning, but the situation had evolved. If Zo and I ended things weeks or months ago, it would not have affected anyone's lives except our own. Now not only would Courtney be affected, but so would the kids. Realizing how it could affect his children made me feel bad. I was finally getting what I wanted, and I wasn't sure how I felt about it.

"I'll keep you updated as things progress, but I just wanted to let you know that I kept my word. I told you I would take care of it, La."

"Okay."

Zo was quiet on his end. I'm not sure either of us knew what else to say, so he changed the subject.

"I can hear that you're in the car," he said. "You on the way to the shop?"

"No. I honestly haven't been feeling that great," I responded. "I told Ayanna that I might stop by urgent care before I go in."

"Urgent care? What's wrong?"

"To be honest, I think I might have a concussion from when I fell and hit my head the other day."

Zo released a frustrated sigh. "You mean when your crazy ass brother pushed you to the ground?"

I sighed as well. "Yeah ... that," I said. "I don't know if he's ever going to be okay with this ... us being together. He hasn't been back to the house since he left the other morning. He won't call me back either."

"Yeah, we've only spoken about work, but I think he'll come around. We've been friends too long for him not to forgive me."

"The fact that you've been friends so long is probably the problem."

"Maybe, but there's nothing I can do about that now," he said.

I pulled into the parking lot of the urgent care facility. "I just got to the place," I said. "I'll call you later."

We said goodbye, and I quickly rushed inside, so I wasn't late for the appointment I made online. After checking in, I only waited a few minutes before I was called to the back to meet with a physician. She greeted me with a pleasant smile.

"I'm Dr. Rhodes. What brings you in today, Ms. Woods?"

"I fell a couple of days ago, and I'm not sure if I suffered a concussion," I told her.

"Tell me what's been bothering you," she said politely.

"Headache ... dizziness ... nausea and vomiting," I explained.

Dr. Rhodes nodded in acknowledgment with an inquisitive look on her face. "Tell me more about the fall you sustained."

I spent the next couple of minutes talking with the doctor and describing the fall and the symptoms I was experiencing.

"I certainly understand your concern, and we're going to get you all checked out," she said standing up. "I'm going to have you leave a urine and blood sample with the lab so we can run a few quick tests. Those are definitely commons symptoms and signs of a concussion, but I want to rule out a few other things."

"Sure."

I followed the doctor to another area of the facility where I did the things she asked. After leaving the requested samples, I was directed back to an exam room to wait. While I waited in the exam room, I thought about my earlier conversation with Zo. There were so many things I neglected to consider when we crossed the line to something more than friendship. Although sleeping with Zo was a conscious decision, at the time, it felt like the inevitable progression of the relationship that we shared. Although we were just supposed to be friends, it felt like something more to me – long before we became involved. I found out it felt like more than friendship to him as well on the night of my twenty-fifth birthday.

. . .

My HEAD WAS SPINNING FROM THE AMOUNT OF ALCOHOL *I consumed. Somehow, I made my way across the VIP club section to Zo and the guys without twisting my ankle in my stilettos. Zo sat on top of the sofa between Nick and JB with his feet resting on the cushions. He looked good – damn good. Zo had always been sexy to me, but something about him that night was causing a dizzying reaction. I don't know what it was, but from the fitted cap that sat on top of his low-cut waves to the retro Jordan 1s on his feet, he had my attention. Too bad my night was coming to an end.*

I reached Zo, placing a hand on his knee and leaning closer so he could hear me over the loud club music. I also purposely gave him a close-up view of my cleavage in the curve-hugging mini dress I wore.

"I'm glad y'all were able to make it tonight," I said to him. "I really appreciate y'all showing love for my birthday."

"Of course," Zo said with a wink. "We not gonna stop showing up for you just because your brother's not here. You should know me better than that."

I smiled in response. Marcus had been in prison for a couple of months at the time. I pulled away from Zo for a brief moment before leaning towards him again.

"I just wanted to come over and thank you for coming ... and all the bottles," I said. "My girls and I had a really good time."

"Then my mission was accomplished. You're welcome."

Something about the smile tugging at his lips and the look in his eyes caused a chill to run up my smile. I fought hard to not reveal the impact he was having on me.

"I'm about to go," I said.

"Back to your girls or home?"

"Home."

Zo looked at his phone to check the time and then back at me with a questioning frown. "Why? It's not even that late."

I shrugged my shoulders. "I had fun, but I'm a little worn out. One too many drinks. I'm trying to get Porsha to take me home."

"Nah. It's cool. I got you."

I hesitated. "You got me?"

"I got you," he repeated. "Tell your girl she can stay and have fun. I'll get you home if you're ready."

"You sure?"

"Positive."

I stood back up and made my way over to Porsha. I knocked back one more shot than I probably should have before saying goodbye. When I walked back over to Zo, he was dapping up his boys and telling them he would get up with them the next day. He stood in front of me, looking me up and down in a way that made me feel exposed.

"You ready?" he asked, placing a hand on my waist. I nodded. "Let's go."

He reached for my hand and led the way out of the club. He held the door open for me to climb into the passenger seat of his truck, and we started the ride with nothing but the sound of the radio playing quietly. When we reached a red light, he turned to look at me.

"You good?" he asked, reaching over to gently rub my thigh.

I smiled weakly and nodded. I was, but I wasn't. I had thoroughly enjoyed my night, but I missed my brother. Since our mother and uncle passed, it was just the two of us. Being without Marcus on my birthday was hitting me heavily.

Zo looked at me with concern as the light turned green. He pulled off from the intersection with his eyes focused on the road ahead. "Yeah. I miss that fool too," he said as if he were reading my mind.

I settled back against the comfortable leather seat and quickly dozed off. I woke up minutes later to Zo patting my leg after parking in front of my apartment building.

"Come on, Sleeping Beauty. Let me make sure you make it in okay."

I hopped out of the truck and Zo motioned for me to lead the way while we started towards my building. After taking the elevator to the fourth floor, we headed for my door. Still a little tipsy, I fumbled around in my purse for my keys, almost dropping them before I could successfully unlock the door. Zo followed me inside. I walked over to the refrigerator and grabbed two bottles of water, handing one to him.

"After all those drinks, we could both use some water."

"Yeah," he agreed, licking his bottom lip.

He took the bottle with his left hand but reached for me with his right. I was caught completely off guard when he pressed his lips against mine. We had flirted back and forth for years, but I never thought anything would happen. Stunned, I hesitated briefly before kissing him back. We both dropped our bottles of water, wrapping our arms around each other. Zo held me so close that I could feel the unmistakable bulge growing between his legs. I parted my lips, accepting his tongue into my mouth while we continued to kiss. A few moments later, I pulled away abruptly.

"Zo ..." I called his name breathlessly.

"Yeah, La ..."

"What about Courtney?"

"What about her?"

I couldn't tell if the look in Zo's eyes was due to desire or intoxication. Either way, I leaned in to kiss him again. A few seconds later, he pulled away when his phone started to ring in his pocket. He kept a hand on my waist but answered his call.

"Aye Nick ... yeah man ... yeah, she's good. You know ... long night. Too many drinks ... Bet. I'll hit you up in the morning."

Zo ended the call and put his phone back in his pocket. I reached for him again, grabbing his shirt and pulling him towards me. When our lips met this time, Zo lifted me off my feet. I wrapped my legs around his waist while he carried me down the hall to my bedroom. I kicked my heels off before he placed me down on my feet. We undressed each other quickly before backing up towards my bed. Zo sat on the edge of the bed, pulling me between his legs. My eyes couldn't help but stretch wide at his length and thickness. I was overwhelmed.

Zo leaned back on his elbows while I lowered myself onto his lap, purposely sitting on his thighs instead of his dick. I hesitated, looking down at the veiny monstrosity that was pointing straight up at the ceiling. Subconsciously, I folded my arms to cover my bare breasts.

"What's wrong, La?" Zo asked, rubbing my thighs gently. *"You don't want it?"*

I shook my head. "No. It's not that. It's just ..."

My voice trailed off while my eyes focused on the weapon between his legs again. I doubted I could take it all, but that wasn't the reason for my hesitation. I forced myself to look into his eyes again.

"... your wife ... my brother. I don't know. I just ... I want this, but I feel like we're about to pop the lid off of something that can't be resealed."

Zo shook his head, rubbing my thighs again before moving to my ass where he gently massaged my cheeks.

"La, my marriage is dead. Don't worry about her, and as far as your brother ... we'll cross that bridge when we get to it," he said. He sat up a little straighter, kissing my lips before he said, "and fuck whatever lids you talking about. I don't give a shit about bustin' it open. Alana, I want you. Can I have you?"

I nodded slowly, and Zo unfolded my arms. He took one of my breasts into his mouth, sucking on it before flicking his tongue across my hardened nipple. He did the same thing to the other one before moving his mouth to my neck where he sucked on it while placing a hand between my legs, fingering my wetness. The sensation of him rubbing my clit was too much. I almost came in his hand. My back arched, and I wrapped my arms around his neck while I squirmed in his lap.

My eyelids felt heavy while he continued to suck on my neck and asked, "Can I feel you, La?"

"Yes," I moaned with my eyes closed.

Placing his hands underneath my ass, Zo easily lifted me up. For a brief moment I held my breath, thinking that he was about to slide me on top of him. Much to my relief, he stood up and turned around – opting to lay me on my back. I ran my hands over his tattoos, admiring the muscles of his chest and abdomen. Zo leaned down to kiss me. With his lips still on mine, his hand traveled between my legs again, sliding two fingers inside. A moan escaped my lips while he moved his fingers in and out until they were coated with my juices. I was dripping wet. Knowing he had me where he wanted me, Zo removed his hand. Looking directly into my eyes, he positioned himself between my separated legs, holding the tip of his dick to my opening before penetrating me slowly.

"Ahhh," I cried, gripping his shoulder while he slowly moved back and forth, easing deeper inside of me. "Oh my God ..."

My body tensed from the pain of each slow and deliberate movement. I tried to relax, but each stroke felt as if he was going to split me in half. One of my hands grabbed his arm while the other gripped the back of his neck, pulling his body down onto mine.

"You good?" he asked.

I nodded, but the look on my face must have said otherwise.

"Lala, you sure?" Zo asked, still stroking me slowly. "You want me to stop?"

I shook my head. "No ... please ..." I said between ragged breaths. "Don't stop, Zo. Please ... don't stop ... "

It took a few more minutes before I could relax and start to feel more of the pleasure and less of the pain. I saw a flash of excitement in Zo's eyes when he felt the tension leave my body. Interlocking our fingers, he slid my hand above my head on the bed while he gave me hard, long strokes. When he eased up on the pounding he was giving me, I raised my left leg, placing it on his shoulder and allowing him to enter me at a different, deeper angle. I started to rotate my hips in a way that caused him to apply direct pressure to my clit. I grabbed at his arms, probably scratching them, as I was unable to control the moans that were coming out of my mouth – moans that sounded more like screams – in between me shouting his name. I'm sure my neighbors would think he was trying to kill me if it wasn't for the banging of my headboard against the wall. I somehow managed to keep my eyes open long enough to watch Zo kiss the calf of the leg resting on his shoulder before his eyes rolled towards the ceiling.

"Shit ... shit Alana ... fuck!"

Zo breathed heavily and pushed my right leg down into the mattress, driving into me as deep as he could. This wasn't a normal after club, intoxicated fuck. No, this was something deeper. I could tell from the way he looked into my eyes and called my name. This was exactly why I hesi-tated. The metaphorical lid had been popped off, and this was the phys-ical release of the pent-up sexual frustration between two people who would have gotten together much sooner if there weren't other factors in the way. I had messed around and fell in the middle of some shit I wasn't sure I could escape.

My body started to tense again.

"Oh my God ... Zo ..." I moaned.

My back arched as I rode the wave of a second orgasm, clawing and scratching at Zo's body. His breaths became shorter and his body more rigid. I could tell he was close as well. I dropped my leg from his shoulder and wrapped it around his waist before pulling him close, so we were chest to chest. I licked his neck and gently bit his ear. That sent him over the edge.

"Uggghhh shit!"

Zo's body jerked while he groaned and released inside of me. Out of breath, his body collapsed on top of mine. After our heart rates returned to normal, he rolled onto his back beside me. For a moment, we laid there in silence, Zo playing with my hair and kissing my face while he held my naked body close to his. It wasn't long before he was reenergized and recharged. He kissed my cheek and then spoke into my ear.

"You think you can ride it?"

We both laughed.

"There's only one way to find out," I answered, climbing on top of him.

When we were finished, the sun was coming up. I laid on his chest while he wrapped an arm around my body and kissed my forehead. The room was quiet except for the buzzing of his cellphone on the floor in the pocket of his jeans.

"Do you need to get that?" I asked.

Zo shook his head. "Nah," he said, rubbing my back. He laughed and said, "But I could use some of that water."

I laughed before getting up from the bed. I paused to pull on an over-sized T-shirt and walked to the kitchen. I grabbed bottles of water and returned to my room where Zo was snoring. I shook my head and laughed again. After sitting the water down on my bedside table, I turned off the lamp and climbed in the bed next to him. A couple of hours later, I opened my eyes to see Zo putting on his shoes while he sat at the foot of my bed fully clothed. I slowly sat up, wincing from the soreness all over my body. Pulling my knees up to my chest, I leaned against my head-board. Zo looked over his shoulder at me.

"Good morning," he said.

"Good morning."

He got up and walked to my side of the bed.

"JB hit me up a little bit ago. Some shit's going on with work. Long story short I have to shower, change, and meet up with Deuce," he explained. "You busy today?"

I shook my head. "Nope. I cleared my schedule at the salon, and PO told me to enjoy my weekend. Maybe just lunch and shopping with my girls."

"Bet."

Zo's phone vibrated, and he paused to check the message. "Yeah. I gotta head out," he said, reaching into his pocket.

I watched while he pulled a rolled wad of money and sat it on my bedside table. My eyebrows arched with attitude.

"Lorenzo Lacey, I swear to God if you leave some money on my nightstand like I'm some goddamn hooker I will – "

Zo started to laugh. "La, chill. It ain't even that. It's a birthday present. Buy yourself something nice, and enjoy your weekend with your girls," he said. He leaned down and kissed my lips. "I know you ain't no ho, Alana. Last night wasn't a mistake either. Happy birthday ... I'll call you later."

I nodded and watched Zo leave my bedroom. I listened for the sound of the front door as it opened and closed moments later. I hesitated briefly but then reached for the rubber band secured roll of money he left behind. I counted the bills to a sum of five thousand dollars. What a hell of a birthday present, I thought to myself. I had no clue what I had gotten myself into.

DR. RHODES ENTERED THE ROOM INTERRUPTING MY thoughts. I quickly searched her face trying to see if I could read anything in her expression. She sat down on her stool and rolled closer to me.

"Well Ms. Woods we've gone over a few things from the lab ... ran our tests ... and tried to figure out what's going on with you," she said with a faint smile pulling at her lips.

A smile.

Good.

I relaxed a little at the thought that maybe I had wasted my time by coming to see the doctor. Maybe there was a stomach bug going around that would explain the nausea and vomiting. I was probably experiencing headaches and dizziness because I had not been able to keep much food down.

"And although the symptoms you mentioned are all common with a concussion, I do not believe that is the cause of your discomfort," she continued. "Ms. Woods it turns out that you are actually pregnant. So, what I would like for you to do is contact your OB/GYN and schedule an ultrasound as soon as possible to determine how far along you are and ..."

Pregnant. *Pregnant?*

I barely heard anything else Dr. Rhodes or any of the office staff had to say. She gave me some paperwork with visit summary notes and suggested follow up on my way out of the office. I was in a daze as I made my way back to my car. I sat behind the wheel for several minutes before even turning on the engine.

My day started with receiving news of Zo's pending divorce, and then this. I had definitely gotten caught in the middle of something I couldn't escape.

❧ 10 ❧
ZO

I tucked my boys into their bunk beds and quietly left their room before heading down the steps on my way to the garage. I paused in the family room where Courtney was curled up on the couch with a blanket while she watched a Lifetime Christmas movie. I grabbed my coat from the opposite sofa and pulled my keys from the pocket. Courtney turned in my direction when she heard my keys jingle.

"You going somewhere?"

I hesitated but then answered. "Yeah. I got some business to handle."

Courtney eyed me suspiciously. "On Thanksgiving?"

I shrugged my shoulders.

"You and I both know that my world doesn't stop for government holidays," I told her. "I spent the day with y'all doing the family thing, but the boys are sleep. I have some moves to make."

"And it can't wait until the morning?"

Courtney tossed her blanket aside and stood up from her seat, walking across the room towards me. Even with a frown on her face, she was still gorgeous. She was tall – about five foot ten, with a slim athletic build from her college volleyball playing days.

She had thick, naturally curly black hair that she had passed on to our boys and a light honey brown skin complexion. It was no surprise she was able to capture my attention so easily all those years ago. However, as I looked at Courtney standing in front of me, I had to admit that I had not felt anything romantic for her in years — despite her beauty. I released a frustrated sigh at her line of questioning.

"I choose to handle it now."

"Whatever, Zo. Run out on your wife and kids like you always do," she mumbled rolling her eyes.

"My kids are sleep. They wouldn't know if I was here or not."

"And of course, you don't give a shit about me," Courtney snapped.

I shook my head, briefly closing my eyes before looking at her again. "I'm not doing this back and forth shit with you tonight."

I turned and started towards the garage door. Courtney followed me, pulling on my arm to stop me from leaving.

"So ...it's just fuck me, huh? You're just going to leave anyway?" she asked.

"Court, what are you doing? Why are you trying to start a fight with me?" I asked. "Asking me dumb ass questions and shit. Talking about I don't give a shit about you. You ain't gave a shit about me in years! You care about the shit I give you. So, let me go do what I need to do to keep that money coming in because you and I both know that's the only reason you're still here."

"I never said that."

"You never needed to. It's in your actions," I responded. "It's always been in your actions. All these years you thought I was cheating on you ... were you more concerned about losing your husband or losing my money?"

Courtney didn't respond. She just stood there glaring at me with her hands on her hips. Her lack of response told it all. Maybe it was my fault for fulfilling her every financial and material want earlier in our relationship, but it had been obvious for a while that money was the reason she stayed.

"Exactly," I said, shaking my head. "You want me to stay here tonight for what? Because you actually want to spend time with me? Or because you fear I may be spending time with someone else ... someone who may eventually get all the material things you hold so dear?"

Courtney dropped her hands from her hips to her sides. The look of anger on her face was replaced by a look I was unfamiliar with her displaying – one that almost looked like sadness.

"I'm your wife and the mother of your kids. Why does it matter how we got here? I may have originally gotten with you because of your money, but that was years ago Zo. I eventually fell in love with you. Isn't that what matters now?"

"You *eventually* fell in love with me?" I smirked. "At least you can finally admit the truth."

"Whether I said it or not you've been holding that shit over my head for years. I don't know why you're so focused on the past. What difference does it make how things started?"

"What difference does it make? Are you serious?" I laughed, shaking my head in disbelief.

"I am serious. I've been trying to work on things between us, but it seems like you'd rather be somewhere else ... or with someone else," she said. "Am I right?"

"Right about what, Court?"

"I've never had any solid proof, but Zo ... I feel like you've been unfaithful for years. Yeah, I know there's money to be made, and you have moves to make, but my God it's Thanksgiving night. You and I both know there's no work-related business that can't wait until the morning," she said. "Am I right in assuming that business is not the reason you're leaving but instead the fact that you'd rather be anywhere but here with me?"

Of course, I wanted to be somewhere else. I wanted to be with someone else for more than just that night. To be honest, I hadn't even done a good job hiding my feelings about my marriage. I was coming home late or not at all, and it was always more important for me to spend time with my sons than Court-ney. However, knowing that I was on the brink of a divorce that was sure to be contested, there was no way in hell I was actually going to admit my wrongdoings to her.

Instead, I looked at her and shrugged my shoulders. Repeating her own words to her, I asked, "What difference does it make?"

The anger returned to Courtney's face, and she shook her head at me.

"Court, you get all the material things you want from me. I take care of this house, and I take care of my sons. Don't worry yourself about what I'm doing or where I'm at when I'm not here with you," I said.

I turned away from her and continued towards the garage door. I paused and looked over my shoulder at my wife.

"Make sure you lock the deadbolt and put the alarm on. I probably won't be back until the morning."

Courtney didn't respond, and I continued to my truck. Hopping in, I cranked the engine and pulled out of the garage. After making a quick stop at the liquor store, I made my way over to PO and Kiara's house. Nick, Alana, and I normally visited with them on the holidays. We didn't want Kiara and the girls to feel any different just because PO wasn't around. The first holiday after losing a loved one is always tough. We just wanted to be there for them. Alana spent the majority of the day with them, helping Kiara cook dinner. After spending part of the day with our parents, Nick left and joined Alana at PO and Kiara's house. I went home to spend a little more time with my sons. Several of the guys had stopped by to check on Kiara throughout the day, and several were still there when I pulled up a little before ten o'clock. Instead of drowning in our grief, we were all gathered together like family kicking it and drinking in PO's memory.

The front door was unlocked when I got there, and I let myself in with bottles of liquor. The main floor of the house was full of friends and family members talking, drinking, and listening to music.

"Took your ass long enough to get here," Nick joked as he approached me.

He helped me carry things into the kitchen.

"Yeah I stayed at home until the boys fell asleep, and then I dipped."

"Courtney at home?" Nick asked.

I shook my head thinking about our conversation on my way out the house. "Yeah, but I don't even want to talk about that shit tonight."

"I understand," Nick said as we reached the kitchen and sat the alcohol down on the counter. "Marcus is around here somewhere, and I don't want to talk about that shit either."

I nodded but didn't respond. Nick had always been closer to Alana than he was to Marcus, but lately, there seemed to be growing tension between the two men. I wanted to stay out of it with hopes that the two men would resolve their issues, and I wouldn't have to pick sides between my brother and my best friend. Aside from my brother, Marcus was still one of my closest friends, even though he was still upset about my relationship with his sister.

"Hey, you finally made it."

I felt arms wrap around my waist and turned around to see Alana.

"Yeah ... took a little while to get the boys to sleep, but I'm here now," I said returning her hug.

Alana gave me a quick peck on the lips before we pulled away from our embrace.

"You want something to drink?" I asked while I reached for a bottle of Crown.

Alana shook her head and raised the bottle of water in her

hands. "Nope. I'm good," she said, "but go on and fix your drink. I have something I want you to taste."

"I bet you do," I said as she started towards the refrigerator.

"And on that note, let me go find Kayla," Nick said, shaking his head and laughing at us. Nick exited the kitchen leaving me alone with Alana and the pecan pie she made earlier in the day. Courtney was absolutely right. I didn't want to be at the house with her. After tasting the pie, I kissed Alana on the lips. I was exactly where I wanted to be with the person I wanted to be with.

ALANA

After a long day of food, alcohol, and guests, Kiara's house finally started to clear out a little after midnight. While some people had plans to continue their night at clubs or other locations, I was ready to climb in my bed. I hugged Kiara goodbye and exited the house, headed towards my car. Zo caught up with me right as I reached my driver side door.

He pulled me into a hug and kissed my neck before asking, "What you about to do?"

"I'm heading home. I know Nick and them said they were headed to another spot, but I'm tired," I answered.

Zo looked tired and smelled of alcohol. I was hoping he would be calling it a night as well.

"What are you about to do?"

"You," he mumbled into my ear causing me to giggle. He tightened his arms around me. "I'm serious. I'm about to say goodbye to Kiara and my brother, and then I'm coming over. Stay up for me."

I nodded. "Are you sure you're okay to drive?"

"Yeah. I'm good," Zo said releasing me from his arms but still standing close. "I'll be over there in a little bit."

Zo kissed me again. When he pulled his lips from mine, I

opened my eyes to see my brother headed towards us. Eye contact had been made throughout the day, but he still had not spoken to me. He had not returned to my home or answered any of my calls since finding out about my relationship with Zo. I was bothered that he appeared to have forgiven Zo but was still upset with me. Marcus walked over to us, and while he greeted Zo, he kept his eyes on me.

"Bruh, what's good?"

Zo shrugged his shoulders. "Ain't shit, man. Getting ready to call it a night. I just need to say bye to Kiara and Nick."

"Calling it a night? I thought you would be getting into these streets with your brother and the rest of us," Marcus finally turned his attention towards Zo.

Zo shook his head. "Nah, man. It's been a long ass day. I won't be getting into anybody's streets," he said. "I'mma let y'all talk while I go say bye. La, I'll be back out in a minute."

I watched Zo's back while he headed towards Kiara's house leaving me alone with my brother. We stood at my car silently for a few moments before Marcus spoke.

Marcus cut his eyes towards me. "So, I guess Zo found something else to get into tonight ... or someone actually."

I rolled my eyes and shook my head, turning to unlock my doors. I pulled on the handle, but Marcus grabbed my arm to stop me.

"What's up, Marcus? You all cool and shit with Zo, but you're still mad at me?" I questioned.

Marcus shrugged his shoulders. "Just because I told him that we're good doesn't mean I'm okay with this. I just needed to get rid of the tension between us so we can work together. I have to deal with him every single day," he answered. "But do you know what that level of betrayal feels like? Do you know how pissed off I was to find out that my best friend has been fucking my sister behind my back for years and that neither one of you told me shit?"

"No, Marcus. I don't," I said, "but you're speaking about this thing between me and Zo like it's some casual fling."

"How should I be speaking about it?" Marcus asked with a frown. "He's married, Alana. He has a wife. You really think he's going to leave her for you?"

I rolled my eyes at my brother. Little did he know that Zo was in fact preparing to leave his wife, but not just because of our involvement. Zo said he should have ended his marriage long before he ever climbed into my bed. Marcus was so sure that my relationship with Zo was a temporary fling, but he had no idea that a child was on the way that would be sure to make our connection anything but temporary. Under different circumstances, I would have shared that information with my brother. However, with the way he was behaving towards me, I chose to keep it to myself.

"Think whatever you want, Marcus. I don't have to defend myself to you," I said turning back towards my vehicle and opening my car door.

"You're right. You don't owe me shit, but you might want to think about defending yourself to Courtney."

I quickly spun around to face my brother again.

"Excuse me?"

"I don't know how you two have been able to keep this a secret for so long because there's nothing discreet about what you're doing," he said. "Her husband is out here buying you houses and shit and kissing you in public. You really think she's not going to find out something? Seems like it's only a matter of time to me."

I glared at Marcus without responding. For a moment, I felt as if he was indicating that he would be the one to reveal the truth to Courtney, but I quickly shook off that thought. Upset or not, I knew there was no way Marcus would ever betray us like that. I was his sister. Zo was his best friend.

"I'm just saying, Sis. What's done in the dark will eventually come to the light. You have to know that."

Of course, I knew that. A child was growing in my womb that would eventually bring the situation to light for all to see.

Although I had not yet shared the news of my pregnancy with Zo, I knew that when the time came, we would take responsibility for our actions together. I wasn't going to beg my brother for forgiveness, understanding, or acceptance.

"Anyway ... I'm out. See you later, Sis."

Again, I rolled my eyes in response while Marcus continued down the street to the Altima. I slid into the driver's seat of my car, but Nick grabbed the door before I could close it.

"Hey," he said holding the door open.

"What's up?"

Nick looked over his shoulder towards Kiara's front door and then back towards me. He sighed before speaking. "Look, I don't have much time before Zo comes back out of the house."

I frowned. "What's going on?"

"Kayla randomly mentioned that she ran into you at the doctor's office the other day, but she didn't get a chance to speak," he said.

"At the urgent care?"

"Nah ... your lady doc's office."

I paused. The day after the urgent care visit, I had an appointment with my OB/GYN to confirm the pregnancy. I knew that if Kayla ran into me in that office that there was a chance she saw me coming out of the ultrasound. I was still in such a daze from the news, I wouldn't have known if she was there or not.

"La ... she mentioned you were getting an ultrasound, and we both know that people can get ultrasounds for all types of reasons," he said, "but ..."

Shit, I thought to myself.

I looked at Nick with a blank stare. "But what, Nick?"

"You know I don't normally get in y'all business ... but I guess all I'm trying to say is that if there's something my brother should know ... you should probably tell him sooner rather than later."

I nodded, but before I could respond, Zo exited Kiara's

house and started towards my car. Nick stood up straight, stepping away from my door.

"Good night, Nick."

"Night."

Nick walked off shortly before Zo reached me. With my door still open, he leaned down into the vehicle.

"You ready to go home?" he asked.

"Yeah, baby. I'm ready."

Zo kissed me on the cheek. "I'm right behind you," he said before closing my door and heading for his truck.

❧ 11 ❧

MARCUS

TWO WEEKS LATER

"All I know is that we better find something out today," JB said shaking his head.

I was shotgun in JB's car riding around on what I considered a dummy mission – an incredible waste of my time. After weeks of looking for Tank, the last remaining member of Prime's New York associates, we had all but given up. The majority of the crew was convinced that Tank had gone back to New York since his whole team was killed and there were no real opportunities for him in Atlanta. However, word had reached Zo that a couple people claimed to have spotted Tank in town. JB and I were skeptical, but Zo refused to let it go. He wanted everyone connected to PO's murder dead, especially Tank since he was their leader. Zo wanted answers, and JB was tired of coming up empty.

I shrugged my shoulders. "I know man. Zo's been kind of relentless with this shit. I'll be glad when this is all over so we can move on to the next thing."

"Right, but Zo's made it very clear that he's not moving on until all these niggas are dead."

96

JB continued to drive. I looked down at the time. I had plans to meet up with someone else that afternoon. I didn't want to waste my day wandering around the city with no results.

"Aye man, where you headed?" I asked.

"To roll up on that nigga Shooter."

I frowned and asked, "Why?"

"Because he's the only one that's been able to give us any halfway decent information. He needs to find Tank too, especially if he wants the rest of this money."

I shook my head and sighed. There was no doubt Shooter would want the rest of the money Zo was offering for information on Tank's location. However, I also knew that even though Shooter helped us find Rome and the rest of the New York crew, I couldn't put all my faith in him. After another ten minutes of driving, JB pulled up to the apartment complex where Shooter lived. He parked, and we both hopped out of the car. I followed JB while he jogged up the stairs to Shooter's front door. JB banged on the door loudly and a few moments later Shooter's pregnant girlfriend, Gina, cracked the door open.

"Hello?" she greeted us with a questioning look.

"We're looking for Shooter. Is he here?" JB asked.

Unfamiliar with us, Gina frowned but started to respond. "He's —"

"G, I got it," Shooter called from behind her.

Gina opened the door wider allowing us into their living room while Shooter walked over to greet us.

"Go on in the back," Shooter told his girlfriend. "This shouldn't take long."

Gina continued to glare at us but didn't protest Shooter's direction. We waited until she was out of earshot to begin our conversation.

"What's up?" Shooter asked sleepily rubbing at his eyes. "I wasn't expecting y'all."

"Yeah I know, but I'm expecting you to be able to make good

on your promise to help us find these dudes from New York," JB responded.

Shooter frowned in confusion. "What? I thought you got them all. I was about to reach out about the rest of the money."

JB shook his head. "Nah. Still trying to find Tank, and Zo ain't offering up shit until he's taken care of."

"I ain't seen or heard nothing about Tank," Shooter responded quickly. "He probably went back up north. What's Zo's deal? Y'all got everyone else."

"Zo seems to believe that Tank is still in town – at least that's what the streets is saying. We made it pretty clear that we wanted anybody that had anything to do with PO's death. If the New York crew was behind it like you claim, then Tank was the leader. He's gotta go just like the rest of them."

Shooter looked at me with expectant wide eyes, but I didn't have anything to say. He looked back at JB and shrugged his shoulders. "What do you want from me, man?"

"For you to earn the rest of this money," JB said. "I want to know this nigga's location by tomorrow."

"Tomorrow?"

"Tomorrow," JB said looking at his watch. "You done already wasted half the day sleeping. Looks like you need to get to work ASAP. I don't care how you get it done. Just get me the information I'm looking for. It's in your best interest to do so."

JB didn't wait for a response. He turned towards the front door and left. Shooter looked at me with raised eyebrows.

"Man, what the fuck?" he asked.

I shrugged my shoulders.

"You heard the man," I answered.

"Yeah I heard him, but come on, Marcus. You got me out here risking my life on some snitch shit when you and I both know that them New York dudes didn't even have anything to do with PO getting shot," Shooter said.

I took a step closer to him.

"First of all, keep your goddamn voice down. What they did

or did not have to do with PO's death doesn't even matter at this point. You told JB and them a story, so you need to continue to sell it. If Zo wants to find Tank, you need to make sure that he's found," I stated. "And let's be very clear, *you* made the decision to risk your life on some snitch shit as you put it. If you were scared, you never should have accepted my offer in the first place."

Shooter shook his head and sighed. I backed up towards the door.

"Find him, Shooter. I don't care how ... just do it or Tank will be the last thing you need to be worried about," I said. "You don't want me to make Zo your problem."

I exited the apartment and jogged back down the stairs to JB's car where he already had the engine running. He drove back to Zo's car wash, where I picked up my Altima and continued towards my next destination. I drove to a 24-hour gym close to Zo and Courtney's house located near the center of downtown Decatur, a small but pricey suburb of Atlanta. I parked not too far from the entrance and spotted Courtney's Lexus truck in the parking lot long before I saw her coming out of the gym headed towards her vehicle. Her schedule was too predictable – something someone in Zo's position should have been concerned about if he was a loving husband. Anybody that had knowledge of her schedule could roll up on her at any time. I exited the car and walked towards her, reaching her at the same time she got to her vehicle.

"Hey," she greeted me with a hug. "What are you doing over here?"

"About to grab lunch at the burger place down the way," I lied as I pointed towards a restaurant in the same shopping center.

"Oh okay. It's good to see you. I know that husband of mine has had you busy since you got home, but you should stop by the house and see the boys some time. I know they were little when you went away, but they still remember you."

"Yeah. I'll do that sometime."

Courtney pressed her key fob to unlock her truck and opened the driver door. "Speaking of the twins, I actually need to go home and shower before they get out of school," she said.

"While you're here, I was hoping I could speak to you about something real quick," I stated.

Courtney tossed her personal belongings onto her passenger seat and turned back around to face me. "Sure. What's going on?"

I sighed heavily, shoving my hands into my pockets. I wanted it to appear to Courtney that I was conflicted to share this information with her. A slight frown came to her face as she watched me put my words together.

"I actually wanted to talk to you about Zo."

The frown lines on Courtney's forehead deepened, and she folded her arms across her chest while leaning against her truck. "What about him?"

I shook my head and sighed again.

"It has to do with my sister."

"Your sister?" Courtney asked. "What does Alana have to do with Zo?"

"I recently discovered that your husband and my sister have been ... involved."

"Involved?"

"Romantically ... physically ..."

"What?" Courtney asked with a look of disbelief. "Marc, what are you talking about? I don't know where you got that from. They're just friends. All of you are friends – you, Zo, Nick and Alana. Good friends. Best friends. Y'all grew up together, right?"

I nodded.

"You're right. We grew up together, but something else apparently started between them while I was locked up."

Courtney silently looked at me, and I couldn't read her expression. I didn't know if she was angry or questioning the truth behind my statement.

"Marc ..." she said shaking her head. "No ... He wouldn't do that."

"He wouldn't do what, Court?" I asked. "He wouldn't cheat on you, or he wouldn't cheat with Alana?"

"Either. Both ... I don't know."

"Look ... I don't enjoy having to tell you this, especially since my sister is the person he's cheating on you with. You know I always thought you were cool, but it seems like I'm the only one willing to tell you the truth," I said. "Be honest, Courtney ... you've had suspicions about whether or not Zo has been faithful for a while. I know there's no way he can be coming home and doing the things that he should be as your husband while he's been carrying on with Alana."

Courtney didn't respond so I continued to speak.

"I wouldn't lie about something like this."

"But why would you tell me this?" she asked with an even deeper frown. "And how do you know? Why should I even believe any of this?"

I shrugged my shoulders. "I'm telling you, because somebody should have told you a long time ago. Apparently, it's not even a secret. They've just been good at keeping it from you," I said. "Zo may be my best friend ... Alana may be my sister ... but it's a pretty fucked up situation if you ask me."

Courtney threw her hands up and shook her head.

"I'm not believing this shit," she mumbled, turning her back towards me.

I gently reached for her elbow before she could climb into her car.

"You should believe it, Court. There's solid evidence of their relationship," I said.

Courtney looked at me with tears in her eyes. I hadn't expected her to cry. I thought she would be angry that Zo was playing her, but I didn't expect sadness. I honestly didn't think she cared about him that much. I wasn't trying to hurt her. My sole purpose was to expose her husband.

"Evidence?" she asked with a raised eyebrow.

"There's a house. A nice newly constructed five-bedroom home in South Atlanta near the Camp Creek Marketplace," I said. I gave her the address. "The house is in Zo's name. When he's not working or with you and the kids, that's where he's been spending a lot of his time."

Courtney bit her lip and angrily wiped at a tear that fell on her cheek. She shook her head looking off into space instead of making eye contact with me.

"Is there something else I need to know about this house?"

"Why don't you just go by there and see," I responded.

Courtney stared at me for a moment before climbing into her truck. Before closing her door, she turned to look at me again.

"On second thought, Marcus. Don't come by my house, and don't come see my boys," she said. "I don't want anything to do with any of you anymore."

Without allowing me to respond, Courtney slammed her door. I stepped back while she started the engine and pulled off. It was unfortunate that Courtney had become collateral damage, but the deed was done. Courtney now had the proof that she desperately sought for years. I knew that she would move accordingly. Zo and Alana were going to find out that their actions had consequences. I knew that Alana's feelings would probably be hurt, but I didn't care as long as it meant her relationship with Zo was done.

12

ZO

I held onto Alana's waist tightly with both hands while driving deep into her from behind. Hearing Alana moan always did something to me. I briefly closed my eyes and bit my bottom lip. Each time I pounded into her the bed shook, knocking against the wall.

"Yes! Ohhhhh yes, Daddy!"

I smacked her ass hard and watched it shake while I continued to dig into her.

"Oh my God ... Zo! Give me that dick, baby!"

I slapped her ass again. Her wish was my command. I grabbed her wrists and held her arms in place behind her back and hit it harder and deeper. Alana buried her face into the pillow to temporarily muffle her screams. She was so tight and was getting wetter with each stroke. I knew I wasn't going to last much longer. I eventually let her arms go choosing instead to put one hand on her waist and use the other to grab a fistful of her hair. I lifted her head from the pillow, pulling her body towards me while I continued to pound into her roughly.

"Fuck!" I shouted.

Shaking my head, I closed my eyes again and tried to fight off the inevitable. I could feel Alana's walls tightened around me and knew it would be a wrap soon.

"Baby ..." she moaned. "Baby ... I'm about to cum."

I let go of her hair, allowing her body to collapse onto the bed. She grabbed the pillow and held onto it tightly. I placed a hand on the small of her back, trying to concentrate on the last few strokes I gave until her body started trembling. Her orgasm caused a ripple effect through my body as I held onto her firmly. I had stopped pulling out a long time ago. I gripped her hips tightly while I came.

With both of our bodies falling onto the bed, I laid on her back for a moment before rolling off to the side. My phone rang, but I ignored it. Alana turned onto her side, staring at me with a satisfied smile while we both attempted to catch our breaths. She rubbed my face, stroking my beard before softly kissing me on the lips. A few moments later, I glanced at the clock on her bedside table to check the time.

"Damn, La. You still on your birth control?" I jokingly asked her. She laughed. "I might have just fucked around and put a baby in you."

I watched the smile fall from her face while she stopped laughing. "Zo ..."

"I know," I said with a sigh before she could say anything else. Shaking my head, I rolled on my back and stared at the ceiling. "I've got a whole situation I need to take care of."

Alana pushed herself up on her elbow to look at me. "No, baby. It's not that ... I –"

She stopped speaking when my phone started ringing again. I reached for it and saw that it was Nick. I silenced the phone and turned back towards Alana.

"What were you saying?" I asked.

Alana sighed heavily and said, "I was about to say that –"

My ringing cell phone interrupted her again. We both looked down at the screen to see Nick trying to reach me for the third time. Alana sighed.

"He probably needs something if he keeps calling you back to back," she said.

Knowing that she was probably right, I answered the phone.

"Hello."

"Damn nigga where the fuck you at?" Nick asked.

"What's going on, man? Why you blowing up my phone?"

"They found Tank."

"Oh yeah? Where?"

"He's been staying at his cousin's grandma house. Somewhere over near the West End."

"Is he there right now?"

"Yeah. JB and Marcus are watching the house. They were waiting to hear from you."

"Shoot me the address and tell them that I'm on my way," I said, cutting my eyes towards Alana.

I watched as she sat up and reached for her robe.

"You sure you don't want them to just handle it since they're already there?" Nick questioned.

"Nah man. I want to try to get some information out of him. He might not talk at all, but it's worth a shot."

"Alright. I'm sending the address now."

Nick and I ended our call, and I sat the phone down. I sat up in the bed while Alana stood up to tie her robe closed.

"What were you trying to say?" I asked.

Alana shook her head. "We can talk later. Sounds like you've got something you need to take care of."

I nodded. "What time are you heading to work?"

Alana shook her head. "I'm not going today," she answered. "I still haven't been feeling that great, so Ayanna told me to take the day to rest."

"You sure you don't need to go back to urgent care?" I asked with a look of concern.

"I'm good. Just tired. It's the holiday season. The shop is really busy, and I've been working like crazy," she answered. "I just need to rest. That's all."

"You sure?"

"Yeah, babe. Hop in the shower. I'll make something for you to eat on the way," she said before kissing me on the cheek and disappearing out of the room.

Because of her former involvement in the business, Alana understood me in a way Courtney never could. She didn't ask unnecessary questions, and she didn't stress me when I had to get up and go. Alana understood that business could take me away from the house at any time. It was a major relief having someone by my side that didn't expect or require me to explain my every move.

After a quick shower, I pulled on some clothes and met Alana in the kitchen. She handed me a bacon, egg, and cheese sandwich and a bottle of water.

"Be safe," she said. Grabbing my crotch, she continued, "And turn your phone off when you get back."

I laughed. "I got you. Get some rest."

I kissed her on the lips and headed out of the door. I hopped into my truck and eagerly started my drive. I was ready to get rid of Tank and put the nightmare of the last couple of months behind us. Murdering PO was an unforgiveable act, and Tank was the last person responsible. I would be able to sleep easier at night knowing that I had gotten rid of everyone who played a hand in PO's demise.

About fifteen minutes later, I pulled onto the street where JB and Marcus were located. I shut off my engine and walked over to JB's car, climbing into the backseat.

"What do you know?" I asked. "Has there been any movement?"

JB shrugged his shoulders. "Apparently it's just him, the grandmother, and two kids," he answered. "The kids are at school, and we haven't seen Tank or grandma come outside."

"What do you want to do?" Marcus asked. "We running up in there or what?"

I shook my head. "Nah. I don't want to bring granny into it unless we have to. I have a little bit of time to wait."

I sat patiently in the backseat. Marcus and JB chatted about sports and other things. I barely paid attention to their conversation. I had tunnel vision. I had no interest in who beat who in the game the night before. All I cared about was taking care of Tank and wrapping up this matter for good. Wiping out the people behind PO's murder weighed heavily on me. True, Aaron and Luke had been pressing me for answers, but I wanted them as well. I wanted to know why. PO was one of the most laid back, unproblematic guys I knew. Of course, he would handle anyone who had wronged him, but he didn't create unnecessary problems for himself. He was heavily respected. He didn't have a lot of enemies. We took action based off the information JB was able to get from the streets, but there was a part of me having trouble accepting the motive I had been given. I was having a hard time believing that the real reason Tank and his crew took out PO was because of Prime's murder. It had to be something deeper. There had to be something else that I didn't know about.

Half an hour later, Tank came out of the house. Surprisingly he paid little to no attention to his surroundings. He hopped in his car and pulled out the driveway of the house we were watching.

"Follow him," I instructed JB.

Without question, JB pulled off and discreetly followed Tank's car. We eventually ended up at a loft downtown. I assumed this location was the place he actually resided. With the remaining members of his crew deceased at the hands of my team, I didn't expect him to be meeting up with anyone – not anyone I would consider a threat anyway. Tank parked and exited his car. He started across the parking lot to his destination.

"Leave the engine running," I told JB while exiting the vehicle.

Again, Tank moved without paying much attention to his

surroundings. I quietly moved behind him, following him while he made his way towards the building. A couple carrying groceries entered the building after Tank, and I blended in behind them. Tank turned down a hallway, and I watched as the couple made the same turn – making things even easier for me. I glanced around casually looking for any security cameras while I continued to follow the group in front of me. I saw none and shook my head in disbelief. I was surprised he would stay at a place with such poor security. Tank stopped at a door while the grocery carrying couple continued down the hall. While Tank fumbled with his keys, I stopped behind him with my back towards the couple who was now letting themselves into their own unit.

Tank quickly found the right key and was sticking it in the lock when he heard the sound of me taking the safety off of my nickel plated 40 caliber pistol. He froze in place.

"Open the door and step inside."

Tank unlocked the door and stepped inside of the loft. I followed him and used my foot to push the door closed. With his hands raised, Tank slowly turned around to face me and sighed.

"I guess it was just a matter of time," he said.

I shrugged my shoulders. "I guess so."

"Well shit man, go on and get it over with," he sighed. "You're wrong ... but go ahead and do what you came to do."

"I'm wrong? How so?"

"Come on, Zo. Why in the world would I take out PO?" Tank asked. "If my whole reason for being down here was to make some money, why would I kill the man that could make it happen?"

"I was hoping you would tell me. I haven't been able to make sense of it all."

"Because there ain't no sense to be made," Tank responded. "We didn't do it. Didn't have anything to do with it at all."

"So, tell me why I heard differently?"

"Because you've got snakes on your team."

"Snakes, huh?"

"Yeah snakes and that boy Shooter knows all about it," Tank responded.

"Shooter?" I asked with a frown. "That's your boy."

"But he supposedly started working with one of your boys. He's the one that told this lie about me and my crew," he said. "If I wasn't busy trying to avoid you, I would have already got rid of his ass. He started all this shit."

I shook my head at the mention of Shooter. Tank was right. Whether Shooter was telling the truth or not, he was definitely in the middle of everything. He was the one that provided my guys with the information about the very crew that he used to work with. Either he was lying to my crew, or he was snitching on his own. Any way I looked at it, Shooter had now become another problem added to the long list of things I needed to handle. I thought I was finished with the whole situation once I took care of Tank, but now Shooter had become my number one priority. For the first time, I was starting to question the accuracy of the information we received. I was going to have to go see about Shooter in person.

I pulled a pair of gloves from my back pocket, sliding them on before I chambered a round.

I looked up at Tank and shrugged my shoulders. "The problem is ... at this point it doesn't matter if Shooter is telling the truth or not. You're a loose end, man. I gotta tie it up," I stated.

"I know, man. I know."

I raised my gun and pulled the trigger once sending a bullet through the middle of Tank's forehead. I quickly concealed my weapon and left Tank's loft. I jogged down the hallway towards the entrance and crossed the parking lot to JB's waiting vehicle. He took off as soon as I slid into the backseat.

"You handled him?" JB asked.

I nodded. "Yeah, I handled him," I answered taking my gloves off, "but we ain't done."

JB frowned. Marcus turned around to look at me.

"What you mean?" Marcus questioned.

"Something feels off. I'm not sure I'm really buying this whole motive behind their actions. I'm not sure how much of the story I believe altogether."

Marcus sighed heavily. "Come on, man. All them niggas is dead. You not gonna get to the bottom of the motive now, and what does it matter? They took PO out, so we struck back and got rid of their whole crew. What else is there to do?"

I stared at Marcus, hesitating briefly before responding to him. I was the boss. I was the man in charge only answering to Aaron Mercer, the head of the Cartel himself. Marcus was close to me like a brother, but he was trying my patience. Knowing that there was still a little tension between us due to the situation with Alana, I decided to answer his question, but I wasn't going to continue to go back and forth with him.

"Before I call Aaron Mercer and tell him that I took care of it. I need to be sure that I took care of the actual shooter," I answered. "Look, you and JB don't need to help me with this if you don't want. I'll go see Shooter myself."

"Shooter?" JB asked.

Marcus released a frustrated sigh and turned around in his seat to face the road ahead.

"Yeah ... Shooter," I told JB. "His name has been mentioned one too many times with some shit that's not adding up. What better way to get answers than to go to the source?"

"I guess," JB responded while shrugging his shoulders.

"Like I said I ain't about to force y'all to do shit. This ain't about taking out a whole crew anymore. I can handle Shooter solo."

JB shook his head. "Nah man. If you think he might be on some snake shit, I ain't about to let you handle that by yourself. I'm with you for whatever just let me know."

"Bet."

JB cut his eyes at Marcus, who remained silent. I smirked but didn't respond. I was just fine moving forward without him, but something was going to have to give. I didn't give a shit if Marcus never accepted my relationship with his sister, he was going to have to respect my position. Moving forward, I knew that I wasn't going to have much more patience for any resistance from him.

❧ 13 ❧

ALANA

"La, what the hell?" Porsha asked. "You haven't told Zo?"
I sighed and ran my fingers through the big curls in my long hair. Leaning back in my desk chair, I looked at my best friend and shook my head. After finishing her day at work, Porsha stopped by the salon to see me and catch up. She was surprised to learn that she was still the only person I that knew about my pregnancy.

"No. I haven't," I answered.

Porsha leaned forward in her chair. "Are you going to tell him?"

"Yes. Of course," I answered quickly. "This isn't something that I can hide. We're going to have a baby."

"Right ... so why haven't you told him yet?"

I shrugged my shoulders.

"I think I just needed time to process the whole situation. Let's be honest ... this isn't an ideal at all. Although Courtney's about to get divorce papers, they're still married. The timing is fucked up," I answered. "Marcus is still being an asshole about everything. The baby is just an added level of stress to an already complicated situation."

"I understand what you're saying ... but they both love you,"

Porsha said. "You're his little sister, Lala. Marcus is going to come around. He might not be happy about how things came to be, but he can't stay mad at y'all forever. It may be delicate timing with Zo finally ending things with Courtney, but that man loves you."

"I know."

"So ..."

"I'm gonna tell him, Porsha. I'm just looking for the right time," I told her. "I was going to tell him the other morning when I took the day off, but he had some shit going on with work and had to leave. He's been a little busy since, but I'm going to tell him. Maybe this weekend."

"Okay so –"

"No enough of that," I said shaking my head and waving her off. "Do you want me to shampoo your hair real quick? I know that's probably the real reason you stopped by."

Porsha lips pulled into an innocent-looking smile. "Sure, friend. If you could fit me into your busy schedule, I would love a quick shampoo and style."

I rolled my eyes at her and we both started laughing.

"Come on girl."

I got up from my desk and motioned for Porsha to follow me out to my station. Although I was mostly focused on the behind the scenes details that went into running the salon, I still took a few appointments, and I always had time for Porsha. After finishing her hair, Porsha and I chatted for a little while longer before we both decided to leave. Porsha, an elementary school teacher, had lesson plans to work on, and I wanted to go to sleep. First-trimester fatigue was kicking my ass. Confident that my keyholder could close the salon by herself, I grabbed my things and walked out with my best friend. We reached our vehicles, which were parked near each other.

"You know I love you, Lala. I'm going to be in your corner through whatever, but there's nothing for you to be scared of," Porsha said. "Tell that man about the baby, so I can share my excitement publicly. You know I can't hold water that long. This is killing me."

"Yeah, I know."

We both started laughing again. Porsha was known to be chatty and a bit of a gossip, but I knew she would never tell my secret. I also knew that she was right, and I needed to relay the information to Zo sooner rather than later. I had already been holding on to the secret for a couple of weeks.

I hugged my best friend and got into my car to leave. On the way back to my house, I was lost in consideration about what the future might hold. A light rain started before I could make it home, and I thought about how well I planned to sleep that night with the rain as background noise. When I got to my house, I pulled the car into the garage and killed the engine. Neglecting to close my garage, I grabbed my bags and hopped out. I was preparing to place my key in the lock when I heard a woman call my name.

"Alana!"

The sun had started to set. Even though the rain was coming down much harder than before, I still had decent visibility. However, I wasn't expecting any company, and I didn't take kindly to unannounced visitors. I stuck my hand into my purse, touching my .38, before I turned around to see who was calling my name.

"Alana!"

There was an uneasiness that settled in my stomach when I saw Courtney close the door to her truck that was parked at the bottom of my driveway. Without an umbrella, she quickly jogged towards me, stepping into my garage without being invited. The quick jog in the rain had drenched her and the rolled-up papers that she held in her hand. She threw the papers at me, which hit my chest before falling to the ground.

"I found these in my house," she said.

I glanced down and removed my hand from my purse so I could pick up the papers. I unrolled the stack to see that it was a copy of the settlement statement for my house – the house Zo purchased – and a copy of the Warranty Deed, which listed both my name and his as co-owners of the property.

I was speechless.

I knew there was no way that Zo would be careless enough to leave the paperwork lying around. Courtney must have known about the house and went looking for evidence. If she knew about the house, there was no telling what else she might have known.

Dammit, I thought to myself as I gripped the papers, rolling them back up. I hadn't spoken to Zo since earlier that morning. I had no idea what he might have known about this situation.

"He's smart ... that man of ours. It definitely took a couple days of searching for me to find this," she said.

I just looked at her. I had no idea what to say. I didn't know what to expect from her. Since she threw the papers at me, it was obvious that she was angry, but I wanted to know the reason for her popup visit. Surely she didn't drive across town to show me a copy of papers I already possessed. I didn't know how to address her until I knew why she was really there, so my mouth remained closed while I looked at her expectantly. I knew that I was in no position to be indignant, but she was the one that had come to see me.

Courtney's glare was intense and hard. She looked like she had more things to say, but her mouth wasn't moving. The rain was coming down harder. With the wind blowing, there was a cold, wet breeze drifting into the garage. Courtney had another ten seconds to say something before I escorted her back to her Lexus and went inside my house. Her light sweater and leggings were soaked. I knew she didn't plan on standing outside much longer either. Suddenly her facial expression softened, and she let out a deep sigh.

"Look, Alana ... I just want to talk for a minute. That's it," she said. "Can we step inside?"

I hesitated. I couldn't think of any logical reason why I

should let my married boyfriend's wife into my home – no logical reason at all. I looked back down at the papers in my hand and then looked back into her face. The anger that had previously been present was replaced with sadness. I contemplated her request. She didn't seem to be a threat. She was considerably taller than me, but she couldn't have worn more than a size four. She didn't have a purse with her, so I doubted she had any weapons. Something in my mind was telling me that if all she wanted was answers to some of her questions that maybe I owed her that. I sighed heavily.

"Come on," I said motioning for her to follow me into the house.

I closed the garage and let us into the house. When she stepped inside, she awkwardly walked through the mudroom and into the kitchen unsure of where to go. I closed the door and motioned for her to follow me towards the kitchen table in the breakfast nook.

"Is it okay if I sit down?" she asked.

I nodded, and she took a seat at the table. I sat across from her on a stool at the kitchen island. A few moments passed without either one of us saying anything. I knew the situation was probably just as uncomfortable for her as it was for me. She looked as if she had no idea how to start the conversation she wanted to have. So, I asked her a question instead.

"How did you find out about the house?"

The anger returned to Courtney's eyes as she quickly looked up at me with a frown. "Does that even matter?" she asked.

I shook my head.

"No. I suppose it doesn't."

There was more awkward silence. I was tired, and this was uncomfortable for both of us. I just wanted to answer her questions and send her on her way. I wanted nothing more than to climb into my bed. My phone started to ring, interrupting the stillness between us. Without looking, I knew it was Zo, but I didn't answer.

"That's him, isn't it?"

I remained silent. I let her inside so we could talk, but I didn't think that answering that particular question was going to help the situation. I still could not figure out why she was really there.

"Look, Alana ... I already knew about you. I mean ... I didn't know that it was you in particular, but I knew there was someone else. I suspected it for years, and then he all but confirmed it on Thanksgiving. So, you don't have to lie to me. I wouldn't be over here if I didn't want to know the truth," she said. My phone started to ring again. "You can answer your phone. He's probably just going to keep calling anyway."

I paused before reaching into my bag and pulling out my cell. I let it go to voicemail. Then I immediately sent him a text telling him that I couldn't talk but that I would call him back as soon as I could.

"Whose idea was it to buy this house?" she asked looking around at my furnishings.

I shrugged my shoulders. "He wanted me to have a safe, nicer place to stay while my brother was locked up."

Courtney smirked and then said, "Come on, Alana. Don't try to make it sound so innocent. What you said may be true, but if you two were really just friends he could have helped by moving you to an apartment in a nicer area. He didn't have to purchase this big ass house. He bought this house because you two were fucking."

I sat on my stool quietly. Courtney already knew the truth. There was no point in me providing any more details. From my days in the streets, I knew how important it was to know someone's motives to determine whether or not they were a potential threat. I was still waiting for Courtney to get to the real reason behind her unannounced visit to my house.

"Things might be rocky between us, but I know my husband. He's a grand gesture kind of guy," she said. "I bet he probably bought that Chanel bag sitting on the counter too."

I looked at her silently.

"I figured as much," Courtney said. "So how long has this thing between the two of you been going on?"

"Three years," I answered without hesitation. I wanted to get it all out on the table so she could get out of my house.

Courtney took in a sharp breath. Her jaw tightened, and I swear I thought I saw her eyes watering. A look of confusion came to my face. I had no clue what was happening.

After a few moments, she shook her head and said, "You've only been in the house for about a year ... I thought ... I just thought ... this was a fling."

"But you said you've known for years that −"

"Yeah, I've known for years that something was going on, but I didn't know it was you the whole time!" Courtney turned her head to avoid looking directly at me. I was almost certain she was crying. "My God ... you two have been hiding in plain sight and doing dirt this whole time. You've been in my house ... around my kids. The whole time telling me you were friends − supposedly best friends. Who the hell does something like that?"

I didn't have an answer for her. There was no justification I could form that she would want to hear.

"He's a decent enough guy and a great father. I just thought he had problems keeping his pants up, and I thought he was messing with multiple, random women. I thought he was messing with women that came and went over time but three years?! That's not a fling. That's a relationship."

She wasn't telling me anything I didn't already know. I knew that my situation with Zo was a lot of things but a fling was not one of them. I hadn't been known for having the most successful relationships, but my bond with Zo was not something I could or wanted to walk away from − especially with the most recent developments.

Courtney turned to look directly at me.

"I went by the salon to confront you there. I was going to publicly humiliate you just like you've done me, but you were leaving when I pulled up. So I followed you here," she said. After a slight pause, she shook her head and continued, "But now I'm not sure why I even came over here. There's not anything that you could say that I would want to hear."

A feeling of guilt troubled me again. Courtney pretty much confirmed to Zo that she had married him for his money, but he was still her husband. However, she was crazy as hell to have followed me home. She knew my background and that I grew up with Zo and Nick. She had to have known that in addition to the gun in my purse, there were several more in my home. She had no idea what she could have walked into by confronting me at my house. However, I also realized that she had followed me to my front door, and I didn't even notice. I was slipping. I was so tired and lost in my thoughts that I hadn't been paying attention to my surroundings. In my past, that could have easily been a huge mistake – sometimes a fatal one.

"This whole time I was sitting here thinking he was just messing around with someone ... you know playing around on the side, but he actually cares about you. That's obvious," she said looking around my house again. "He's not frivolous with his money."

I sighed heavily. She still wasn't telling me anything that I didn't know. I wouldn't have continued the relationship for that length of time if I wasn't sure how he felt about me.

"I don't know what to tell you," I said with a shrug of my shoulders.

Courtney looked at me with tear-stained cheeks, but her glare was angry again. "I wouldn't think that you would."

I shook my head. "Seriously, Courtney," I said. "What do you want from me?"

Courtney stood up from her chair. Immediately, I became defensive while I watched her cross the room to where I was sitting. She stopped a little less than a yard away from me.

"Alana, I love my husband, okay? Yeah, we may have our fair share of problems, but when I married him that shit was for better or for worse. Obviously, you're the worse in this scenario," she said.

Although I'm sure her words were meant to draw a reaction from me, I bit my tongue and remained silent. She was probably right anyway. In her eyes, I was the worst thing to happen to her marriage.

"Finding out that he was messing around with you damn near killed me, and I initially came over here to ask you woman to woman to leave him alone," she said, "but now ... knowing what I know and how long this has been going on ... now ... you can have him. I'm sure in the divorce I'll get more than what is owed to me for his wrongdoings and for me to take care of our children. Enjoy my leftovers, Alana. You two whores deserve each other. It seems like you and your mother have a lot in common ... you know besides the whole crackhead part."

I shook my head and let out a deep sigh. I may have been in the wrong for sleeping with her husband, but there was no way I was going to allow her to speak ill of my dead mother and disrespect me. If I didn't know I was pregnant, I would have slapped the taste out of her mouth.

"Courtney, I understand you're upset, but I let you in so you could get whatever information you came all the way over here for," I said looking back up at her. "What I'm not going to do is let you sit here and talk crazy to me in my house."

"A house that my husband paid for."

"My name is on the deed right along with his."

Now I was the one with the hard, angry stare silently challenging Courtney to say something else crazy. She didn't, and our conversation was over. It was obvious that things were about to take a turn and go sideways. It was time for her to leave. I slid off the barstool and told her, "I think it's time for you to go."

Courtney hesitated but took a step back. She followed me to the front door, which I held open for her. She stepped into the doorway, but then she paused and turned back towards me.

"Nice car," she said. "Did he ...?"

"Yep."

"Hmph," she said shaking her head and stepping back out into the rain.

I closed the glass storm door and watched as she walked back to her truck. I stood there while Courtney climbed into her Lexus and backed out of my driveway before closing and locking my front door. I leaned against the door – releasing a deep breath and closing my eyes for a brief moment. Then, I stormed back into my kitchen. Digging through my Chanel bag, I grabbed my cell phone and dialed Zo's number.

"Hey babe what's going on?" he answered quickly.

I shook my head in disbelief. "Your wife just left my house."

"What?"

"Yeah ... need to talk."

I heard Zo sigh heavily before he said, "I'm on my way to you now."

❧ 14 ❧
ZO

Courtney flipped through the divorce papers while I quietly sat across the kitchen table from her. I had purposely waited until the boys were at school to come home and talk to her, but there was no point in delaying things further. After her visit to Alana the day before, there was nothing left to hide. Everything was out in the open. There was no more pretending that Courtney and I were something we were not. We had not been *happily married* in years. It was time to officially bring our marriage to an end.

"I'm not leaving this house," she said as she continued to look over things.

"I wouldn't ask you to," I answered. "Keep reading."

We sat in silence while Courtney finished looking over the paperwork. When she was finished, she neatly stacked the documentation and pushed it away from her towards the center of the table.

"What the fuck is this?" she asked angrily.

Confused, I narrowed my eyes at her. "I don't understand your question."

"I guess you just have it all figured out, huh? I suppose this is what you would call fair?" she asked. "I get the house, a decent amount of assets, more than enough financial support, and primary custody of the boys."

"I think it's more than fair," I responded. "What's the problem?"

"I want more."

"More?" I questioned with a frown. "I'm giving you a lot, Court. What exactly is more?"

Courtney shrugged her shoulders. "I don't know. I just feel like this isn't enough," she said pointing to the paperwork. "You maintained another relationship for almost half of our marriage. I feel like this arrangement you want me to agree to lets you off easy."

"Lets me off easy? How am I getting off easy when I'm giving you primary custody?"

"Oh please! You were going to give that to me anyway based solely off of your lifestyle and how you make a living. You aren't doing me any favors," she said. "You owe me more than this for all those years you were fucking that bitch you've been calling your best friend. How do I even know if the income you're using to determine support even includes all your little businesses used to clean your dirty ass drug money? You need to go back and talk with your lawyer and figure out what else you can come up with."

"Or what?"

I did not take kindly to being threatened by anyone whether it was an enemy on the streets or the mother of my children.

"Or I'll have people on the other side of the law looking all into your shit to make sure you're not hiding anything from me. Try me if you want to, Lorenzo. I'll leave no stone unturned," she said.

My jaw tightened. I took a deep breath and shook my head before I responded to her.

"I bet that shit sounds good to you, doesn't it?" I asked. "Courtney, look ... I understand that you're upset about Alana, but you already said that you knew there was someone else. You shouldn't have been so surprised. You're trying to fight me about money ... the real reason you've stayed around all these years – not for me or the kids. I'm giving you more than your fair share of money. Take some time to think about things and consult your lawyer, but it's within your best interest to agree and sign so we can both get this shit over with."

Courtney looked at me as if she thought I was crazy. I continued to speak.

"I'll have the majority of my stuff out before the kids get home from school, and we can talk to the boys at a time you agree to and let them know that daddy won't be staying here anymore," I said, "but when it's all said and done you're going to sign the papers, Courtney. If you start looking into shit that doesn't concern you or turning over stones as you put it, the outcome won't be good for either of us. What type of sense does it make for you to have anyone looking into any potential illegal activity on my part? What the hell do you think you're going to get if I end up in prison?"

Courtney folded her arms across her chest and looked away from me. She didn't have an argument to make because we both knew that I was right.

"Whatever, Zo."

I stood up from the table. "If we're keeping it one hundred, neither one of us should have stayed in this marriage as long as we did, but at least something good came out of it – our boys. Hopefully, you won't hate me forever," I said shrugging my shoulders. "At least now you're free to find someone you truly love ... hopefully, someone that will love you back."

She turned to look at me, but she didn't respond to my statement. I left her alone in the kitchen and went up the stairs to start packing some of my things. Not too long afterwards, I heard the front door open and close. Courtney was leaving to go to the gym. I spent the next couple of hours packing. Since I was leaving Courtney with the house and all the furniture, I only needed my clothing and a number of other personal items – all of which could fit into the cargo van Nick drove to the house.

"Is that everything?" Nick asked after he put the last box into the van.

"Everything that matters right now anyway," I said shrugging my shoulders.

"So what's up now?" he asked. "Where are we taking this stuff?"

I gave Nick a look that let him know he should have known the answer to his question. Alana and I had already discussed it the night before, but it shouldn't have been a surprise to Nick that I was taking my things to her house.

"My bad," he laughed. "Are you ready to head over there?"

"In a minute. What you got going on later?" I asked. "I'm trying to see if you want to ride somewhere with me and JB."

Nick shrugged his shoulders. "I'm free. What's good?"

I leaned against the back of the cargo van. "We're trying to find Shooter."

"What for? I thought we were done with all that New York shit. I thought Tank was the last one."

I shook my head. "I don't know. Maybe. I'm just trying to get a few more questions answered."

I filled Nick in on the information from Tank, and how it sounded a lot like what Rome was trying to tell us before Marcus put a bullet in his head. There was a strong possibility that Rome and Tank worked together to create an alternate theory on what happened in an attempt to spare their lives. There was also a chance that they were telling the truth. The thing that stood out in my mind was that neither of them gained anything from PO's death. It was all casting a bit of doubt in my mind, and I wanted to be confident on what was truth and what was a lie before I met with Aaron Mercer the following week.

"So you're questioning the information Shooter originally gave us?"

I shrugged my shoulders. "I don't know, man. That's what I'm trying to figure out. It sounded good at the time, but he had strong financial motivation to tell us anything."

"I told you something wasn't right about him," Nick said. "I told you that man seemed a little shady."

"You did, and you might be right. That's what I'm trying to figure out," I said.

"Bet. I'll be ready to ride whenever."

MARCUS

I pulled the Altima into Alana's driveway and killed the engine. I hadn't been back to her house in weeks. Since finding out about her relationship with Zo, I knew it would be better for us all if I stayed somewhere else. JB was friendly with a leasing agent at an apartment complex in Midtown and had been able to pull strings to get me a place. After telling Courtney about Alana and Zo, I knew it would only be a matter of time before their marriage completely imploded. When that happened, I knew Zo would work his way into my sister's house if she would allow it. I had hoped that sending Courtney to Alana's house would have put an end to my sister's relationship with Zo, but it did not turned out that way.

Why would he go anywhere else when he paid over a quarter-million dollars for that piece of property? In my opinion, Alana was too blinded by the things he did for her to see him for who he really was. He could have easily just given Alana the money so she could purchase the house herself without him being tied to it. Instead, he purchased the home and added her name to the deed. It was technically his house. He always had a way of controlling things.

I didn't know if Courtney was going to tell either one of them how she found out about their situation, but I didn't care about that either. I just needed to get the rest of my stuff out of my sister's house without being bothered with her or Zo. With it being the middle of the day, I figured I would easily be able to get in and out of the house without running into anyone. I hopped out of the car and made my way to the front door. My phone started to ring as soon as I put the key into the lock.

I shook my head when I looked at the screen and saw Shooter's name, but I answered the phone anyway.

"What's up man?"

I closed and locked the door after entering the house. I started up the stairs towards the room that held my things.

"Man, I'm trying to get my stuff together to get out of town until Zo let's this thing go, but I have to make sure my granny is going to be straight. I need the rest of that money."

I sighed as I stepped into the room. I put the call on speakerphone while I started to gather my things.

"I'll get you the money as soon as I can. I have to go back to my source. I'll have it to you no later than next week. Until then you need to lay low because Zo is looking for you. He's still looking for answers."

"Why is he looking for me?" Shooter asked. "I told them boys everything you wanted me to tell them. I even found Tank like you told me to. I don't understand what the problem is."

"Zo's starting to think that something's not right with the story. He's starting to doubt that the New York crew had anything to do with it."

"Then we have a problem, because he's right," Shooter said. "What am I supposed to tell him if he finds me before I can get out of town?"

"I don't know man. I'll come up with something," I told him.

I tossed a suitcase belonging to my sister onto the bed and started to fill it with clothes and shoes she purchased for me when I got out of prison.

"Marcus, you gotta come up with something, man. This was all your idea. You're the one that wanted to kill PO in the first place," he said. "I just went along with your plan for the money. I'm not trying to take the fall for this like I was the mastermind."

I let out a frustrated sigh.

"I know man. I said I'll come up with something. You just gotta lay low for a couple of days before Zo has to head to Miami. I should have your money by then, and you should be able to get out of town before he gets back."

"Alright man," Shooter said sounding equally frustrated. "You've come through so far so I ain't gonna stay on your case about the money, but ... don't leave me out there alone on this one with Zo. You wouldn't have been able to take PO out if it wasn't for me. I didn't even ask you why. I've held up my end of the deal every step of the way. You owe me, man."

"Yeah alright, man. Alright."

I shook my head while I threw a few more things into the suitcase. Shooter was right about the fact that I wouldn't have been able to pull things off while I was in prison if he hadn't been on the outside helping me. He was wrong about one thing though. All I owed him was the remaining money I promised him. Now that Tank was taken care of, and all of the New York crew was killed, Shooter's job was complete. I would try to buy him time with Zo. I gave him the heads up to get out of town, but once I gave him his final payment he was on his own.

"Look man, I'm kind of in the middle of something. I'll hit you up if there's anything else I have to tell you. If not, I'll be in touch to get you the money."

Shooter agreed, and I ended the call. Finished with packing my things, I grabbed the suitcase and turned to leave the room. Alana was standing in the doorway with tear-stained cheeks and anger in her eyes. She was barefoot in a robe with her hair pulled into a bun on top of her head. She hadn't gone into work that day. She was home the whole time I was on the phone. I shook my head knowing that since I had the call on speakerphone, she had probably heard everything.

"Lala ..." I sighed.

"What did you do?" she asked quietly with fresh tears spilling from her eyes.

I sat the suitcase down and took a step towards my sister.

She jumped back, holding her hands in front of her defensively and looking at me like I was a monster.

"La, I don't know what you heard ..."

"I heard everything, Marcus!" she yelled. "What the fuck did you do?"

I paused before I answered her. There was no point in trying to lie to her if she had already heard my conversation with Shooter. Still, I knew she wasn't going to like or understand anything I had to say. I shrugged my shoulders and shook my head before looking into her eyes.

"I did what I had to do."

"What? What the hell does that mean, Marcus? You did what you had to do? You killed PO? How is that something that had to be done?" she yelled at me. "We're talking about PO! We wouldn't have any of the things we have if it wasn't for him and Uncle Darrell."

I took another step towards her, but she pushed me away.

"You don't know the whole story," I told her evenly.

"It doesn't matter what your story is! Nothing you can say can make this okay," Alana said. "That man was like family to us ... Kiara ... the girls."

Alana shook her head and turned away from me. I reached for her arm and turned her back around.

"He wasn't your family, Alana. I am – just me. Not PO, Kiara, the girls ... and not your boy Zo," I told her firmly. "When it comes down to it, no one is going to look out for us the way we look out for each other. PO may have helped us get our start out in the streets, but he wasn't loyal to us like family should be. He wasn't the saint you made him out to be."

"What is that supposed to mean?"

"He was the man behind Uncle Darrell's murder," I said. Alana's face twisted into a frown. I could tell she didn't believe me. "He didn't pull the trigger himself, but he was the one who set it up."

Alana shook her head. "No. I don't believe that. They were best friends."

"Ain't no friends in these streets, La."

"I'm not buying that ...

"Apparently, Julian favored Uncle Darrell over PO, and he wanted to be the man behind the man. He set his best friend up so he could one day be the man in charge."

"What? Marcus, that doesn't sound anything like the PO we knew for years, but even if it were true why didn't you tell me or Zo?"

"You're having a hard time believing me right now. Do you think that Zo would?" I asked. "As far as Zo is concerned, PO walked on water. PO is the same man that put him in position to eventually run the whole organization – a position I should have had. A position that would have been mine if I never went to prison."

Alana narrowed her eyes at me in a questioning manner. "So, what is this really about, Marcus? Did you have PO killed because you truly believe he had Uncle Darrell set up? Or because Zo got something you thought should be yours?"

I paused again. The truth of the matter is that both reasons were motivating factors behind my actions, but there was no way I was going to tell her that. Given the nature of their relationship, I knew she would not be able to keep that information from Zo. I did not want to run the risk of her telling him something like that. If Zo knew how I truly felt about his rise to power, he would figure that I would be after him next.

"It's because of what he did to Uncle Darrell."

"Then you need to tell Zo," Alana said. "If he really had Uncle Darrell killed, then you need to tell him before he finds out what you did. He'll probably understand."

I shook my head at her.

"No."

"What do you mean no?" Alana yelled.

"Lala, he's not going to understand. PO meant as much to Zo

as he did to you. It doesn't matter what the circumstances were. He's not going to understand, and he can't find out."

"So, you want me to lie?"

I took another step towards Alana, and this time she didn't back away. I placed my hands on her shoulders.

"He can't find out, La. No one can."

Before she could open her mouth to respond new tears sprung from her eyes.

"Marc, Zo and Courtney are getting a divorce, and he's going to be living here. That's why I didn't go to work this morning. He's probably on his way over here right now," she said. "What you're asking me to do is a lot. I don't know if I can do it."

"You have to," I said, shaking her shoulders. "I'm your family, Alana. Everything I've ever done for you our whole lives ... your loyalty should lie with me."

Alana jerked away from me. I took a deep breath and stepped back into the bedroom to pick up the suitcase. I wanted to be long gone before Zo showed up. I returned to the hallway where Alana was still glaring at me.

"He can't know, La. PO is gone. It's done. Telling Zo ain't gonna fix that. It's just going to make things more difficult for you and me," I told her. I kissed Alana on the cheek. "Pull yourself together before he gets here. I'll call you later."

I didn't wait for a response. I figured she didn't have anything to say anyhow. I jogged down the steps and out of her house. I was hopeful that my guilt trip about loyalty would be enough to keep her mouth shut.

❧ 15 ❧

ALANA

"Looks perfect," Sharon James, Porsha's mother, said after looking at her hair in the handheld mirror I gave her.

Sharon passed it back to me, and I sat it down so I could remove the cape from around her neck. Sharon smiled and reached for her purse, digging through it and pulling some cash from her wallet. She handed me the money and stood up from the chair.

"Christmas is less than two weeks away, Alana. Porsha told me that your brother is home. Do you two have plans?" she asked with a warm smile. She had always been kind to us.

I shrugged my shoulders.

"We don't have any plans set in stone right now," I answered.

"Well you know you're always welcomed at our house," she said. "We're going to have a lot of family over and a ton of food. We would love to have you join us."

"I appreciate it. I'll check with Marcus. Even if I end up doing something, I'll still try to stop by," I truthfully told her.

"Sounds good. Hopefully we'll get to see you both."

I hugged my best friend's mother and walked her to the front of the salon. When I reached the door, Zo was on the other side, opening the door to step in. I gave him a surprised look. I had no idea he was stopping by. He held the door open for Sharon, who said another quick goodbye before walking outside.

"Hey," I greeted Zo with a smile after he stepped inside of the salon. "What are you doing here?"

"Just trying to catch up with you. We've been busy the last couple of days," he said. "I was trying to take you to dinner if you had time."

Zo was right. We had both been busy since he moved his things to the house, which was also the same day I found out about my brother being behind PO's murder. Zo had been busy tracking down someone else he thought had something to do with it, and I had made myself busy at work. By the time he was getting home at night, I was already asleep, and I would be gone to work in the morning before he woke up. I was still looking for the right opportunity to tell him about the pregnancy. In addition, I had to keep my knowledge of Marcus's actions to myself. Holding in both secrets was becoming too much for me. It was easier to avoid him, but that was hard to do when we were living under the same roof.

"Yeah," I said with a forced smile. "That will work. Maria and India have late appointments. I'm sure they'll be fine closing by themselves."

Zo leaned in to kiss my cheek. "Cool. Grab your things so we can go."

I stopped to speak to two of the stylists about closing, which they quickly agreed to, and then headed back to my office. After I shut down my computer, I slipped into my coat, grabbed my purse, and headed back towards the reception area where Zo was speaking with Ayanna. The two were pulling away from a friendly embrace when I joined them.

"I'm on my way out too," Ayanna said to me. "What's for dinner?"

Zo shrugged his shoulders. "Whatever the boss wants," he said motioning towards me.

"In that case ... I'm thinking steak ... a really big one," I said.

We all laughed.

"Zo, it was so good to see you," Ayanna said. "I'll let you two enjoy your evening. Alana, I'll see you in the morning?"

I nodded. "See you in the morning."

Zo held the door open for me while we exited the salon. Once outside, he took my hand and started towards his Range Rover.

"Ride with me, and I'll bring you back for your car."

We got into his truck, and he made the short drive over to STK Steakhouse. After being seated quickly, we placed our orders and chatted until the food came.

"So work's been pretty busy lately, huh?" Zo asked.

I looked up from my glass of water and smiled across the table at him.

"Very. Christmas is right around the corner. Everyone needs their hair done before family time," I answered. "Next week will probably be even more insane."

"Damn babe. I thought one of the benefits of living together was that I would actually get to see you more," he said before taking a sip of his beer.

"It's temporary, but I think it's cute that you miss me," I said with a wider smile.

Zo laughed and shook his head. "Yeah, whatever. Calling me cute and shit. I'm a grown ass man."

I laughed and reached across the table to hold his hand.

"I'm sorry. You're my sexy fine ass man."

"You better know it," Zo said while he winked at me.

The waiter brought our food, and we started to eat. Moments later, Zo spoke again after taking a bite of his creamed spinach.

"I've been looking forward to waking up next to you in the morning, but honestly I've been trying to give you something for the last couple of days."

I raised an eyebrow and licked my lips seductively. "If we're both heading home after this meal, you can give it to me tonight."

Zo shook his head and laughed again. "That ain't what I was talking about, La," he said taking another sip of his beer, "but thanks for making my shit hard at the dinner table."

"Oh ... my bad," I laughed. "I'll take care of that when we get back to the house, but what were you talking about?"

Zo reached into the pocket of his coat and pulled out a slip of paper. He slid it across the table to me. Chewing a bite of my NY strip, I wiped my mouth and hands before picking up the piece of paper. It was a balance statement for a bank account. My eyes traveled down to the bottom of the slip of paper and zeroed in on the total amount of money that was in the account – a very large amount of money. I looked back up at him.

"Zo, what is this?"

"You remember the joint account we opened before we bought the house?"

"Yes," I answered, "but we haven't used that account since the closing. Why is there so much money in there?"

"It's an early Christmas present," Zo answered. "I know this Christmas is going to be a little different with Marcus home but not really around and me moving in but still needing to split the holiday with Courtney and the boys. I still got something else coming for you, but I wanted to give you this first before the real holiday madness starts."

"Zo ... that's a lot of money."

"Enough to buy the salon from Ayanna?"

My eyes lit up. "Yes. Definitely. That's enough to buy the salon twice."

Zo shrugged. "I didn't have exact numbers," he said. "Keep the rest and buy something nice for yourself. You deserve it for putting up with my shit for so long."

"I'll drink to that," I jokingly said while I reached for my glass of water.

"Let's get you a real drink. Red or white?" Zo asked for my preference in wine while he looked around for our waiter.

I shook my head.

"No, it's okay. My water is fine," I said waving him off.

"You sure?"

"Yeah. You know me. I have no self-control when it comes a good red wine," I rambled. "I'll drink a whole bottle and be hungover in the morning. Can't do that. I actually have a number • of appointments scheduled for tomorrow. The next two weeks I'm doing more hair than usual."

Zo settled back into his seat and shrugged his shoulders.

"Suit yourself," he said.

"Thank you, baby," I said looking back down at the account statement. "I don't know if I can thank you enough. I mean ... this really surprised me. I can't believe you would do this."

Zo sat up in his chair again leaning forward in my direction. "Believe it, Alana. I would do anything for you," he said. "I told you that I got you. I got us. You should know that by now. At least I hope you know that."

I nodded and smiled at him. I believed every word he said. It felt like the perfect moment to finally tell him about the baby. Right as I started to open my mouth, our waiter came by to check on us. As soon as he walked off, Zo's phone started ringing.

"My bad," he said as he fumbled with the volume on the phone. "I meant to put it on vibrate. Shit, it's actually Luke."

"It's fine. Take your call. I'm just going to continue eating this delicious ass steak," I told him.

"Alright. Hopefully this won't take that long," he said while standing up and pressing the phone up to his ear.

I watched as he walked away to take the call in private. The perfect moment had passed, but I knew I needed to tell him soon. I couldn't continue to hold onto both my secret and Marcus's. It was too much.

NICK

"He's not here," Shooter's girlfriend, Gina, said. "I told y'all that already!"

I shook my head and looked over at Zo, who had a frustrated look on his face. JB came from one of the back rooms in the apartment to join us in the living room.

"That nigga ain't here," JB said.

"Nah man," Zo said.

"That's what I told y'all before y'all forced y'all rude asses in here," Gina spat.

I ignored her, but silently wished that she would shut the hell up. Nobody was going to have any more patience for her mouth. Zo frowned and turned towards Gina.

"Where is he?"

Gina rolled her eyes. "Are you niggas deaf or stupid?" she asked. "I told you he wasn't here."

JB started in Gina's direction, but Zo held up a hand for him to stop. JB glared at Gina angrily but backed up.

"You said he wasn't here, but you didn't say you didn't know where he was," Zo responded. "The nigga's car is out front, and one of my people said they just saw him not too long ago. He couldn't have gone far."

Gina folded her arms across her chest.

"I don't know where he is."

Zo shook his head and laughed. "Come on now. There's no way you can really think I would believe that. You're his girl, and you're pregnant. You really expect me to think that he would leave home without telling you where he was going?"

"Maybe he knew y'all would come by here harassing me," she said.

"Hmm. Maybe," Zo answered.

I continued to stand to the side while Zo and Gina glared at each other for a moment. I had been riding around with my brother and JB for a couple of days trying to find Shooter. So far, we had come up empty.

"Let's go," Zo said to me and JB even though he kept his glare fixed on Gina.

"Bruh, you know she ain't telling the truth," JB said. "This bitch lying like hell."

Zo shrugged his shoulders. "Maybe she is. Maybe she isn't," he said. "Either way we ain't about to get any information out of her. Let's go."

I rarely questioned my brother, and I knew JB wasn't about to make him repeat himself another time. Although he wasn't really satisfied with the answer, JB knew he wasn't calling the shots. He shook his head but turned and headed for the door. Zo lingered for a moment, still glaring at Gina.

"Next time you speak to him tell him that I stopped by here tonight and that we ain't going to stop looking for his ass," he said. "Tell him he needs to make himself available unless he wants me to continue to harass you and his grandma."

Gina rolled her eyes again but didn't respond. Zo walked towards the front door, and I followed him out of the apartment. We jogged down the steps of the apartment building to the parking lot where JB was waiting by Zo's truck. We climbed inside, JB in the back and me in the passenger seat, while Zo pulled out of the lot.

"Where to now?" JB asked.

"I'm about to drop you off," Zo answered.

"What?"

Zo sighed. "Look man, I appreciate you riding with me on this one when you didn't have to, but we ain't going to find anything else out tonight. I gotta get home and get ready to head out in the morning."

Zo was headed to Miami to meet with Aaron and Luke.

"Alright man," JB said, "but you know that bitch was lying."

"You're probably right, which is why I want eyes on her and the apartment while I'm in Miami. Get someone on it that can be discreet and keep their mouth shut," Zo said. "Everybody don't need to know my business right now."

JB nodded. "I got you."

We continued our drive without much conversation. After dropping JB off, Zo continued on to my condo building. We sat in the truck for a minute after he pulled into the parking lot.

"You told me something wasn't right with Shooter," Zo said.

I shrugged my shoulders. "I couldn't put a finger on it at the time, but I knew something was off," I responded. "The fact that he's gone MIA is making it even more obvious that he's on some shady shit."

"I know."

"What are you going to tell Aaron?"

"Shit, the truth," Zo answered quickly. "The hell I look like lying to that nigga?"

We both laughed. Aaron and his father, Manny Mercer, always had a way of knowing things – sometimes before they were even told.

"You're right," I said. "You gotta tell him what's up for real. He always seems to find out shit."

"For real."

I hesitated before I asked my next question.

"How's everything going at home?"

Zo laughed and shook his head. "Which home?" he asked. "I knew Courtney was going to eventually sign the divorce papers, but she really didn't put up much of a fight after the day I gave them to her. The divorce will be final sooner rather than later. We worked out a custody agreement for the boys, and she's getting more than enough money. You know that's all she really cared about anyway."

I sighed. "At least that will be over soon like you said. How's Alana?"

"I don't know."

"What do you mean?"

"Something's off with her," Zo answered. "She ain't been

herself lately, and I can't quite figure out what the problem is. I guess I just expected something different once I moved in. To be honest, she's been kind of standoffish. She said work is real busy or whatever, but I can hardly catch her at house. I don't know ... maybe she's just tired. Christmas is right around the corner, and I guess she might be busy or whatever ... but I'm getting a sneaky vibe from her. If I didn't know any better, I would say that she was avoiding me, because she's trying to hide something."

Listening to my brother speak about his suspicions made me think back to Kayla telling me how she saw Alana at the doctor's office and my conversation with Alana afterwards. Alana never confirmed whether or not she had information to share with my brother. It also wasn't my place to hop in the middle of their business. From years of dealing with Courtney and Zo, I had learned to stay out of anything concerning my brother's love life. It didn't have anything to do with me, and I wanted to keep it that way.

"She might still be up when you get home," I said glancing at my watch. "Why don't you try to talk to her about it before you leave?"

"Tonight?" Zo asked shaking his head. "Yeah, I don't know about that. If I'm wrong, I'm not trying to start a fight or an argument before I leave town for a few days. Bro, you know how her mouth and attitude can be. It's been reckless since we were younger. I ain't trying to deal with that right now."

I laughed because Zo was right. Alana and I, the younger siblings of our brothers, were the same year in school. I knew her before Zo did. She had always been known to have a bit of an attitude problem and a slick tongue. It had gotten a little better with age, but it was probably the reason many of her relationships before my brother didn't work out. The guys she dated got tired of her talking to them like she was crazy. She had found her match in Zo. Although I know she still tried it every now and then, he wasn't the type to allow anyone to speak to him the same way Alana had dealt with the men of her past.

"For real, bro. I'm just trying to get in, finish packing, maybe be lucky enough to get some ass, and call it a night," he said.

I nodded and laughed.

"I feel you."

"Alright, man. Let me head on to the house," Zo sighed. "I'll hit you up sometime tomorrow, but you know what it is. Business as usual and keep an eye out for Shooter. If anything happens with that, I want to know the second it's going down."

"Of course."

We said goodbye, and I climbed out of my brother's truck. I headed into the building and took the elevator up to my floor. My phone started to vibrate in my pocket as I let myself inside my place. I closed my door and looked at the screen to see JB calling me.

"What's up?"

"You still with bruh?"

"No. He just dropped me off," I answered. "What's up?"

JB sighed. "This shit with Shooter, man. Something is off about all this."

"Why you say that?"

"We ain't never had no problems trying to locate him until we started to suspect something with him," JB said. "He could very well still be in town somewhere, but let's say that he isn't. Why would he have fled? What would make him think that we were looking for him to the point that he ain't even been home?"

I paused to consider his question. JB had a point. Up until recently, Shooter had been available to us whenever we needed to speak with him. It wasn't adding up.

"You're right, man. It doesn't make sense."

"I know. It makes me think that he knows that we're looking for him," JB said.

"But it's just been you, Zo and me. We ain't involved nobody else," I said. "Right now, nobody else on the team even knows that we're trying to find him."

"Except for Marcus."

I closed my eyes and pinched the bridge of my nose. I let out a heavy sigh. JB was right. Marcus knew before I did that Zo was going to be looking for Shooter. He was the only other person that could have given Shooter a heads up. I had no idea why, but now Marcus looked like he could have been working with the other side – whoever's side that might be. We still weren't sure at this point.

"JB, let me try to get ahold of him and see what's going on. I'll hit you back in a minute."

I hung up the phone and tried to call Marcus. After getting his voicemail twice, I hung up and stared at my phone in disbelief. It wasn't even midnight yet. I knew he wasn't asleep. I thought about calling Zo, but I didn't want to disturb him. Not until I had something solid to tell him.

ALANA

Ayanna's eyes were wide, and even though her hands were clasped in front of her face, I could still see her smile.

"Oh my goodness!" she squealed. "I am so happy for you and Zo! Oh my gosh ... I had no idea!"

Ayanna hopped up from her desk and walked around to hug me. She pulled away from our embrace and touched my stomach gently. She smiled again.

"How far along are you?"

"Almost ten weeks," I answered, "and outside of my best friend Porsha you're the only person I've told."

Ayanna's smile remained on her face, but her forehead wrinkled slightly while she gave me a questioning look. "You told me before you told Zo?"

"Yeah. Long story, but I'm planning to tell him when he gets back this weekend."

"Okay. So ... why me first? What made you come in here to tell me today?" Ayanna asked.

"I actually wanted to talk to you about your proposal to purchase the salon," I said, "but I wanted to be upfront with you about everything. I know you would be turning everything over to me, but this salon is still your baby. You and your sister created this place. I want to take over for you. I feel that I am ready to take over, but with the baby ... I don't know."

Ayanna smiled and motioned for me to sit down.

"Have a seat, Alana," she said.

I sat down in an empty seat in front of her desk.

"Alana, you're the only person who has worked for me that I would feel comfortable handing my business to. Sounds like you just need a pep talk, and lucky for you, that's what I'm here for."

Ayanna was right. I had always been fearless and confident. I rarely doubted myself and was always ready to take on a new challenge. I had been that way my whole life, but this was uncharted territory. This time it wasn't just about me. Being a business owner did not make me nearly as nervous as becoming a mother. Doing both at the first time was making me question my capabilities for the first time in my life.

Ayanna's voice broke into my thoughts.

"Lala, I'm going to keep it real with you. When my father brought you around, I instantly took a liking to you, because you reminded me so much of my sister and me. Our backgrounds and how we were raised may be different, but some things aren't about pedigree – there about DNA. Some things are just ingrained in who you are. Hustle, drive, ambition ... those things can't be taught," she said. "Your skill as a stylist is unmatched, but I've never seen anybody who was able to pick up the business side of things as quickly as you, especially when your knowledge comes from self or on the job training. You're smart as a whip, and that's where I see a lot of me in you. You're also determined as all hell. You don't let anything stand in your way. You overcome any and every obstacle you come across, and that's where I see a lot of Jada in you."

Ayanna laughed and shook her head.

"You know just like I do that Jada doesn't stop. When she decides she wants something, she's like a dog with a bone. Nothing can get in her way. She turned over her businesses in Atlanta to me, because she was going to move to Miami and enjoy life as a stay at home mom. At least that's what she said," Ayanna laughed again. "She's almost seven months pregnant with her second child, and she's diving in headfirst on a new business venture. That's just who she is. She ran three different businesses while she was pregnant with AJ rarely taking any days off because she knew that the success or failure of the business depended on her. You take that same accountability when it comes to how you handle your business. You're already running the salon like it's yours. I don't have to worry about this place when I take a day off, or I'm over at the boutique or the restaurant."

Ayanna paused to look at a picture on her desk of her daughter, Katy.

"If there's anything I've learned from watching my sister or from my own experience, it's that being a mother is not going to set you back, hinder you, or prevent you from being the best businesswoman you can be. If anything, it's going to push you to your greatest potential," she said with a wide smile. "Your baby is going to make you go harder than you've ever gone before because you'll know that your success isn't just for you anymore. It's for your family, and you'll want to do the best you can for them every single day."

I smiled at my boss. I appreciated hearing her words. Having someone else believe in me during a rare moment when I doubted myself meant a lot.

"I know you're more than capable, Alana. You're going to kick ass, and on the off chance that you ever need me I'll only be a phone call away," she said.

"Thank you. I really appreciate it, and I really needed to hear that."

"No problem girl. Anytime," she said, "and whenever you're ready to discuss the purchase proposal I'm ready."

"I'm actually ready now. I thought I might need a little bit of time to get the money together, but I have it all. Zo gave it to me the other night."

Ayanna's eyes widened in surprise while her smile stretched across her face again. "All of it?"

"All of it and then some," I answered. "I already had some of the money saved up and thought he might be able to help me out, but he gave me the money as an early Christmas present."

"And remind me again why you haven't told him about this baby yet?"

Ayanna and I both laughed.

"I know. I'm going to tell him as soon as he gets back in town," I answered. "It's just been so much going on lately. I had to figure out how I felt about everything before I even thought about trying to find the right time to tell him, but I can't hold on to the secret anymore."

"No you can't, and you shouldn't want to either," Ayanna said. "Whether or not the timing is ideal, you two are about to have a baby. That's a beautiful blessing. You shouldn't be going through any of this alone, especially when you have a man at home that loves you."

I nodded. "You're right. You are definitely right about that."

I left Ayanna's office and returned to mine to finish some work before my next appointment arrived. After reviewing the expenses for the month, I pushed my work to the side and reached for my phone. I had not spoken to my brother since finding out that he was behind PO's murder. I was still struggling to make sense of the information I discovered. However, as upset and angry as I was, Marcus was still my brother. I still wanted to make sure that he was okay. I still had a desire to mend the relationship between him and Zo. They were my only family.

I dialed Marcus's number, and he answered before it went to voicemail.

"What's up, La? You good?"

"Yeah. I was calling to check on you. I –"

"I'm kind of in the middle of something right now," he interrupted me.

I frowned. I wondered why he even answered the call if he was just going to rush me off the phone.

"I didn't want to keep you long. I actually just wanted to make sure you were okay. I haven't heard from you, and –."

"I'm good, La. Did you need something?"

I paused briefly while I continued to hold my cell phone to my ear.

"I was trying to see what you wanted to do for Christmas," I stated. "It's right around the corner and we don't have plans."

"Who is we? You talking about you and me? Or you and your boy?" he asked with a laugh.

"I was talking about me and you, but I mean ... Zo will probably be around."

Marcus laughed again.

"Yeah, that's what I thought. Look, if you want to hang out that's cool, but I don't know about spending the holiday with your boyfriend."

"He was your best friend first."

"Exactly. That's why he never should have crossed the line with you," Marcus said. "Pardon me if I don't want to sit here and act like we're all one big happy family."

I shook my head at him. When I had the baby, we were all going to be family – happy or not.

"You can't avoid us forever."

"I'm not trying to avoid you. I'm just not trying to be around your boy unless it's work-related," he said, "but La, I need to go for real. I'll talk to you later."

Marcus ended the call before I could respond. I rolled my eyes and stood up from my desk. One way or the other I was going to have to find a way to rebuild the bridge between the two most important men in my life.

NICK

"Babe, you look a little tired," Kayla said while she rubbed my back. "You sure you don't want to just go home?"

I yawned but shook my head. "Nah it's cool. I'm not that tired, and JB is gonna pull up in a little bit."

I lied. I was tired as hell. Zo would be back in the next day or so and I couldn't be happier. Between looking for Shooter and helping JB with the day-to-day, I had been burning the candle at both ends. Zo had been in his role for a couple of months, and it was time for him to formally assign his number two. I had no desire to do any more than what I was doing in regard to running my trap and handling my own business. Of course, I would always help my brother if he was in a bind, but I never had the desire to follow in his footsteps completely. When it all came down to it, I didn't think I was cut out for it. JB probably could have held it down, but we all knew that it should have been Marcus.

When we were younger, and we thought about the day Julian and PO retired, we all used to picture Marcus and Zo running the city side by side like the men who trained us. However, now that was looking like less and less of a possibility. I didn't know why Marcus was so surprised about Alana and Zo because the two had been flirting for years before anything happened. To be honest, I wasn't sure why Marcus was so upset because Zo was dating his sister. I couldn't figure out if it was because Zo was married when it started, or because neither of them said anything to him about it for years. Whatever the reason, he had a right to own his feelings. I just couldn't believe that he wouldn't let it go. We had been friends for over fifteen years, but the tension between Marcus and Zo was starting to affect business. I was sure that wouldn't continue for long, especially if Aaron Mercer caught wind of it.

I took a sip of my drink and hung my head, closing my eyes for a brief moment. The loud club music was starting to give me a headache. I had been so busy lately that I had barely spent any time with Kayla. That was the main reason I wanted to stay out a little longer before we went back home, but I wasn't sure how much longer I could last. I sat back up and checked my phone to see if JB had tried to reach me. I was relieved when I saw a text from him saying he was on the way in. JB and a few other people we knew joined us in VIP. My plan was that Kayla and I would hang with him and his girl for no more than an hour and then I could head home.

An hour and a half later, I paid the bottle girl and stood up to say goodbye to the group. JB got up and stretched.

"I'm bout to follow y'all out," he said. "I'm tired as hell."

I laughed. "Shit. Me too, bruh."

"I don't see any signs of things slowing down either," JB said.

"Me either," I said, shaking my head.

JB and I followed in behind our women as they led the way towards the club's exit. I shook my head and released a deep yawn. Between my fatigue and the drinks, I was glad Kayla was sober so she could drive. We all made small talk while heading towards our vehicles. As we reached the back of the parking lot something to my right caught my eye. I blinked hard to make sure there was nothing wrong with my vision. I extended my arm to stop JB from walking any further.

"What's up?" he asked curiously.

Kayla and JB's girlfriend, Lauren, stopped walking when they realized we weren't right behind them. Kayla looked at me with a frown.

"Babe ... what's going on?" she asked.

That's what I was trying to figure out.

"Bruh, look over there to your right," I said quietly to JB while our women looked at us with questioning eyes. "You see what I see?"

JB casually looked to his right and his forehead wrinkled in confusion.

"That looks like Marcus. That's definitely his car. I can't tell who he's with though."

I let out a heavy sigh and shook my head. "Dammit man," I mumbled. "Aye, I need you to send Lauren home. She can hop in with Kayla. She'll drop her off at your place."

"What?"

"Look closer, man. He's over there talking with Shooter."

JB's eyes squinted and then opened wide. "You gotta be shittin' me," he mumbled while he approached Lauren.

"Babe, what's going on?" Kayla asked with less patience.

I walked closer to Kayla while JB spoke with Lauren quietly. I reached in my pocket and handed her my keys.

"Take Lauren home, and I'll call you later," I said before kissing her on the cheek.

Kayla still had a questioning look in her eyes but quickly agreed. She knew it wasn't the time or place to get into all the details. I made my way back over to JB while our women took off towards my car.

"You strapped?" I asked JB.

"Always," he answered, "but who is the other guy with them?"

I glanced back over my shoulder. When I initially spotted the group, I could only identify Marcus and Shooter. I wasn't able to get a good look at the third guy at first. I looked a little closer and then shook my head in disbelief. Things were starting to make sense, but I could not believe what I was witnessing. I turned back towards JB.

"That's the guy that shot PO."

JB's face instantly screwed up into a frown while he reached for his weapon.

"Chill. Hold on a minute," I told him, placing my hand on his to stop him from drawing his gun.

"What you mean hold on?"

"What are you about to do? Just rush over there and start shooting?" I asked him.

I was careful not to speak too loudly as people were coming and going all around us.

"Nah," I said. "Just hang on a minute. Shooter is the one that we want. We know how to find Marcus, and if they're all working together, Shooter can eventually lead us back to the triggerman."

JB's nostrils flared and his jaw clenched, but he relaxed his shoulders slightly. He was on board with my plan. I motioned for him to follow me. Without looking directly at the three men in question, JB followed me towards an F-150 in the parking lot that we leaned against and pretended to be engaged in conversation. However, we were really keeping an eye on Marcus and his associates. We watched closely until a few minutes later, when Marcus hopped into the Altima, and the other two walked away in separate directions.

The triggerman got into a car not too far from Marcus, and they both pulled out. Shooter started to walk in our direction. JB and I looked away while trying to remain unnoticed until he passed us, and then we followed him. When he reached the driver door of his car, JB was right behind him with his gun in his hand. I made my way around the other side of the car, pausing by the hood so that he couldn't get away.

Shooter damn near dropped his keys when he looked up and saw us.

"You're a pretty hard man to track down," JB said.

"What you mean?" Shooter laughed nervously. "I've been around. You've been looking for me?"

"Nigga, don't play stupid," JB responded. "I'm sure that loud-mouth bitch of yours told you we stopped by your crib."

Shooter sighed and dropped his shoulders. "Alright, man," he said. "What's going on? What do y'all need from me now? I found Tank and all them New York niggas."

"Yeah we actually have questions about that," I stated, looking at Shooter with narrowed eyes. "However, first I want to know what's in your pocket?"

"What?"

"You took something from Marcus, man. I ain't got time for you to be playing dumb. What's in your pocket?" I asked again.

Shooter stuck his hand in the pocket of his coat and pulled out a stack of cash. I shook my head.

"Go ahead and hand my man JB those keys and hop in the back," I told him. "We're gonna take a ride so we can get some answers."

Shooter released a heavy sigh but followed my instructions. He had to know that there was no escaping at this point. I didn't want to jump to conclusions, but the picture was becoming more and more clear. It appeared as if the concerns I had about Marcus and Shooter were valid. JB and I were going to do all we could to get the necessary answers to our questions. Afterwards, I would call my brother.

Then someone was going to have hell to pay.

☙ 17 ❧

ALANA

My life was nothing close to a fairytale. I was thankful for the things I had gained as an adult, but I had to bust my ass for all of it. With my shitty upbringing and challenges in early adulthood, sometimes it was hard to believe where life had taken me. After years of working in the streets with the guys, I had pursued my passion and become a sought-after hairstylist that was a few short weeks away from owning her own salon. It still felt surreal that I was becoming a legitimate business owner. While I was achieving professional success, I was also finding happiness in my personal life. After numerous and sometimes volatile relationships in my teens and early twenties, I was finally able to continue my relationship with Zo unrestricted by his previous circumstances. Things were finally coming together for me.

Zo's trip to Miami had come to an end, and he was back in town. He sent me a text when he landed to let me know that he was on the way to our home. I quickly lit the last of a few candles in our bedroom before rushing over to check my appearance in the full-length mirror in the corner. I was ready to welcome my man home and tell him about our pregnancy.

I heard the door open and shut and smiled at my reflection

in the mirror. I had just styled my hair earlier that day. I quickly ran my fingers through my long, wand curled hair before opening my short silk robe to display the revealing negligee I wore underneath. I opened the bedroom door and headed to greet Zo, but I was surprised to see him racing up the stairs practically taking them two at a time.

I placed my hands on my hips, showing off my wide smile and all my curves.

"Damn, baby. Where's the fire?" I asked when he reached the top of the stairs, joining me in the hallway outside of her bedroom.

Zo paused. His eyes took in my appearance as he looked up and down my body, but he did not return my smile.

"Where is your brother?" he asked evenly.

I frowned.

"What?" I asked, laughing uneasily. "I'm standing here damn near naked, and you're asking me about Marcus's whereabouts. I don't know."

Zo walked closer to me, and I grabbed his hand in an attempt to pull him into our bedroom.

"Get in here so I can –"

Zo pulled away from me, refusing to be led into our room. I looked at him with a confused smile on my face. I had no idea what was going on with him, but my plans for our evening seemed to be going sideways pretty quickly. I placed my hands on his shoulders, rubbing them gently.

"Babe, I don't know what's going on, but why don't you come –"

Zo grabbed my hands, removing them from his shoulders but holding onto them tightly. His grip was almost painful.

"La, where the fuck is your brother?" he questioned with a tight jaw.

I looked into his face and saw the fiery anger in his eyes – anger that had never been directed towards me. My stomach dropped. He was aware of Marcus's actions.

I struggled to free my hands from Zo's grip before taking a step away from him.

"I don't know where he is. I don't – he hasn't – I don't know. I haven't been invited to his new place yet. I don't really see him like that."

Zo stared at me for a moment with a clenched jaw before sighing heavily and covering his face with his hands. He dropped his hands into balled fists by his side and looked at me, shaking his head slowly.

"Alana ... *are you fucking kidding me?*" he shouted.

"Baby, I ..." my voice trailed off.

I didn't know what to say.

"You fucking knew what he did, and you didn't say anything to me?!"

Zo shouted so loudly that I backpedaled until I was against the wall.

"He's my brother," I said softly.

"And PO was like a father to you. Like a father to both of you! I can't believe you didn't tell me this!" he snapped. "That's not a secret you get to keep! If he could do that to PO, what the fuck do you think he would do to me?"

I was quiet for a brief moment to consider his question. Digesting his words, my stomach became unsettled. I hadn't previously thought about all the potential repercussions of Marcus's actions.

"Zo ... Marcus could never," I said shaking my head. "He would never try to kill you."

"Yeah well, we aren't going to find out because I'm going to put a bullet in him first."

My eyes stretched open wide.

"He's your best friend!"

"Ain't no friends in these streets, Lala. You know that."

"No. I don't know that," I said with tears stinging my eyes. "What about you and me? We were friends first."

Zo shook his head. "I don't fuck my friends."

"Wow."

I blinked hard, cringing at how harshly he described our relationship history. He shook his head and sighed.

"You know what I mean," he said in a softer tone of voice.

I ignored his comment.

"You can't kill my brother."

Zo shook his head again. "La, you and I both know that's not how this works. Not after what he's done."

"What are you saying to me right now? You're the boss. It works however you say it works!"

Zo released a deep sigh and shook his head again. "Look, I'm sorry. I shouldn't have come home like this. I'll call you later."

"Call me later? Where are you going? You're not coming home tonight?"

Ignoring my questions, Zo backed away from me and turned towards the steps. I rushed after him, grabbing his arm.

"What? No ... You can't leave like this!"

Zo turned to face me. "I'm sorry, Alana."

"Don't be sorry. Don't do it!"

"He should have known there would be consequences when I found out."

"Zo, please. You can't kill my brother!"

Zo gently tried to pull his arm away from me. I held on tight.

"I don't know what this is going to do to us," he said with a sad look in his eyes. "I don't know if you're ever going to be able to forgive me."

My tears continued to well in my eyes. I felt frantic while I tried to plead my case.

"All the rest of our family is gone, Zo. He's the only family I have!" I cried.

"Nick and I are always going to be there for you, Lala. Even if you don't want me to ... I'm never going to turn on you, but –"

"You don't understand! I need my brother, Zo. I need my family right now," I cut him off.

Zo looked at me suspiciously before saying, "He was gone for three years, and I was the one that made sure you were straight. Why the hell do you need him right now? What is it I don't understand?"

My tears started streaming down my cheeks. I was losing my composure. This wasn't how I planned to tell him about our baby. After the years of struggling to define our relationship, things were finally working for us. We were finally going to have a real shot at making it. This was supposed to be a happy occasion – something to celebrate that was going to bring us even closer. However, I was on the verge of a nervous breakdown, trying to beg the man that I loved to spare my brother's life. No, this wasn't what I pictured at all.

"What aren't you telling me, Alana?"

"Zo, I ... I'm pregnant."

Zo's eyes rolled towards the ceiling before closing. He shook his head slowly and released another deep sigh. He stuck his hands into the pockets of his pants before opening his eyes and looking at me.

"You're just full of secrets. Aren't you?" he laughed sarcastically.

My eyes widened. That was definitely not the reaction I envisioned.

"What?" I asked, blinking away more tears.

"I guess it makes sense though ... that's why you were the only one not drinking at Kiara's house on Thanksgiving. That's why you stayed home sick from work that day ... and that's why you turned down a glass of wine with your steak the other night. Wow ..." he said. "How long have you known?"

I shrugged my shoulders weakly.

"Don't give me that shit, Alana. You remember exactly when you found out. That's not something that anyone would forget," he said in a frustrated tone. His voice elevated again. "How long have you known?"

"I found out the day I went to urgent care."

Zo reacted with another short, sarcastic laugh. "So, you thought you had a concussion, but it was really a baby."

Emotionally, I was all over the place. The tears kept falling from my eyes.

"That was weeks ago, La. When the hell were you going to tell me you were carrying my child?"

"Tonight. That's why I —"

"That's pretty convenient."

"Excuse me?"

"I'm saying ... you've supposedly known for weeks that you were pregnant, and you don't say a word to me until you're standing here begging me not to kill your bitch ass brother?" Zo questioned. He removed his hand from his pocket and stroked his beard. "That don't look funny to you?"

My eyebrows raised in shock. I was lost for words.

"Get out," I calmly said before I could stop myself.

"I tried to leave a moment ago! I told you I shouldn't have come straight here in the first place," Zo said, turning back towards the stairs.

"Get ... out!" I repeated slightly louder than before.

"Alright, Alana. I'm out. Just make sure that if you see that nigga before I do that you tell him I'm looking for him," Zo said as he started to descend the steps.

"Get the fuck out of my house!" I screamed with tears running down my cheeks again.

I snatched off one of the Alexander Wang stilettos that Zo had recently given me and threw it at him. I watched it hit him in the middle of his back, but he did not respond or react. Moments later, I heard the front door slam and then the sound of his engine starting before he pulled out of the driveway.

❦ 18 ❦

NICK

J B grabbed his gun and his keys and turned towards me.
"You ready?" he asked.

I nodded. "I'm ready to get this shit over with. I'm so glad Zo gave the green light to dead these niggas."

I followed JB out to his car, which was parked in his driveway. After he and I were able to get useful information from Shooter the day before, I immediately called Zo and filled him in on the details. According to Shooter, Marcus was the mastermind behind PO's murder. Somehow, from prison, Marcus got connected with Shooter who helped get a hired gun to facilitate the murder. After wrapping up their business in Miami, Aaron sent Zo back to Atlanta on their family's jet so we could handle business. Zo instructed JB and I to get rid of the triggerman and Shooter while he dealt with Marcus.

"You know what Zo's going to do with Marcus?" JB asked as we climbed into his car.

I shook my head. I knew what should happen with Marcus. It was the very thing that Zo wanted to do, but Alana complicated the matter. I imagined that Zo killing his girlfriend's brother could put a strain on their relationship. However, Zo had always taken care of business without letting personal relationships cloud his vision. This would be his first real test as the boss.

JB sighed and continued his drive. From Shooter, we had learned that the triggerman was some career criminal named Eric. No one on our team was too familiar with him, but he supposedly made his living by stealing and killing. Shooter gave us an address for Eric, and we were headed to find him. Several minutes later, JB pulled onto a quiet street of single-family homes. With the sun setting and very minimal street lighting, we were able to watch the house in question discreetly. JB had a history of being trigger-happy and typically didn't have a lot of patience. As much as I know he wanted to run up in Eric's house shooting, we both paused when we noticed two cars in his driveway.

"What do you want to do?" I asked.

"Sit for a minute and see if his company comes out or if there's any movement."

We sat in the darkness of his vehicle for an hour or so until we saw the front door open. Eric walked a woman out to her car and soon she pulled away from the house, driving out of the neighborhood. We watched Eric walk back into the house and close the front door. JB turned towards me.

"You ready?"

I nodded. "Let's go."

Gripping our weapons, JB and I exited his vehicle and walked around the back of the house. JB was able to pick the fence lock quickly, and we entered the backyard and headed for the rear door. Confident that Eric was alone in the house, we wasted no time kicking in the back door. I was surprised that there was no active alarm system. Eric rushed into the kitchen with his gun drawn only to be met with bullets from both JB and myself. He was able to let off a few shots, but they missed us. We struck him in the shoulder, arm, and leg before he fell to the floor.

"Shit!" he yelled.

Eric laid on his back gripping his wounded shoulder while his blood started to spill onto floor. JB and I walked closer to him. Eric shook his head and grimaced while he looked into our faces, seemingly recognizing who we were.

"I told Marcus that Zo was going to figure it out. I should have known this was a suicide mission," he said through gritted teeth.

JB shrugged his shoulders. "Yeah you should have known," he said before he raised his weapon again and shot Eric in the face. He paused and turned back towards me. "Let's get out of here and handle that other matter."

I agreed and followed JB back to his car. He put his car in drive and started towards our next location. I was ready for the night to be over so we could get back to business as usual. Once Zo decided how Marcus would be dealt with, we could put it all behind us. Nearly half an hour later, JB pulled into the parking lot of one of Julian Reid's old warehouses. We hardly ever used the space, but it came in handy every now and then due to its seclusion. Recognizing the other car in the parking lot, I knew that the necessary members of our crew were already inside waiting for us.

We entered the warehouse to find the familiar faces of our crew – people who worked particularly close with JB as his "cleanup crew". Also present was a bloodied and bruised Shooter, tightly bound to the chair he sat in. Sweat and blood dripped from his forehead towards his swollen, blackened eyes which he was able to open wide enough to recognize the presence of JB and myself.

"Nick ... JB ... come on man. I did what y'all asked ..."

He grimaced as he spoke. I would not have been surprised if the men had broken his jaw when they roughed him up. I stared at Shooter with no emotion whatsoever. His begging did not affect me at all. He had a lot of nerve to even hope for mercy. He showed no mercy for PO. He ended his life for less money than I make in a week. I could not even comprehend why he would imagine I would show him mercy when he helped facilitate the murder of the man who had been a mentor to me for a long time.

JB shook his head and turned towards me.

"You got this, or you want me to do it?"

"I got it."

I pulled my Glock 40 and put in a new clip before I aimed the gun at Shooter. He mumbled a few more pleas, but I ignored his requests. I squeezed the trigger over and over until I was out of bullets. I looked at Shooter's lifeless body with satisfaction knowing that I had ended the life of one of the men responsible for taking PO's. JB took the gun from my hand and handed both our weapons to his cleanup crew. I listened while he gave instructions to dispose of the weapons and get rid of Shooter's body. I exhaled deeply feeling relieved that as soon as Zo came up with a plan for Marcus, we would all be able to sleep peacefully for the first time in months.

After JB finished giving his instructions, I grabbed the stack of money that was sitting on a nearby table – money Shooter had received from Marcus. Then we headed back to JB's car. He put the car in drive and took off from the warehouse.

"One last stop."

We rode in near silence – nothing but background music – until JB pulled into the familiar parking lot of an apartment complex. He put the car in park but left the engine running while I opened the passenger door, grabbed Shooter's money, and hopped out. I climbed the stairs two at a time until I reached the top and then quickly made my way to the door of the person I was there to see. It was late – a little before one in the morning – but I would knock on the door until the person answered. A few moments later, Shooter's girlfriend Gina opened the door with a frown on her face.

"Do you know what time it is?" she spat. "I don't know what the hell you're doing here! I told you last time that I didn't know where he was. I haven't talked to him in a couple of days!"

"I know. I'm here to give you this," I said, extending the money in her direction.

Gina hesitated and looked down at the money with questioning eyes.

"What? Why are you giving me this?"

I pulled the money away from her. "If you don't want it, I can take it with me."

"No ... no. I can use the money. I want the money," Gina said, "but why are you here to give me money at almost one o'clock in the morning?"

I sighed and handed the money back towards her.

"Look, just take the money for your baby and his grandma."

"His grandma?" Gina eyes widened. "Where is he? Where is Shooter?"

I shrugged my shoulders.

"I don't know. You don't know. Hell, as far as I'm concerned you don't know me either. You've never seen my face. Do you understand?"

Gina nodded slowly. I continued to speak to her.

"I'm serious, Gina. Taking this money means you've never seen me or anybody I work with. If anybody asks, you have no idea what could have happened to Shooter," I told her. "You can report him as a missing person if you want to, but you have no knowledge of anything. Are we clear?"

Gina nodded again.

"Crystal clear."

"Good."

I placed the money in Gina's hands and turned to walk away. My phone buzzed in my pocket on the way back to JB's car. Zo sent a text telling me he was heading to my place.

"Where to?" JB asked.

"Back to my spot," I answered. "Zo's headed there now."

"Did he find Marcus?"

"I don't know."

I shook my head and settled back into my seat until we reached my condo.

ZO

Nick and I sat on the stools at the breakfast bar catching up on the events of the last forty-eight hours. Nick and JB had been able to take care of their business, but I had come up empty. I picked up my beer and took a sip.

"Was he there?" Nick asked.

I shook my head and sat my beer bottle back down on the bar in front of me. "Nah man. He wasn't over there, and she said she doesn't know where he is either."

"Dammit man! Where the fuck is he?" Nick asked with a frown.

I shrugged my shoulders.

"I don't know man, but I'm looking for his ass. I told his sister to tell him."

"Oh shit! You told Lala about it?"

"She already knew."

Nick frowned. "What the fuck do you mean she already knew?"

"She knew, man," I said before taking another sip of my beer and shaking my head. "And guess what else?"

"What?"

"While begging me not to shoot that motherfucker she tried to tell me I can't kill him because she's pregnant and she needs her brother."

Nick downed his whiskey and sat the empty glass down. "Damn ... So, she finally told you, huh? Good. That's a weight off me, bruh."

I cut my eyes at him.

"You knew she was pregnant?" I asked with questioning eyes.

Nick raised his hands defensively.

"To be honest I wasn't really sure what was going on," he

said. "Apparently, she and Kayla have the same lady doc, and Kayla saw her at the office getting an ultrasound. I spoke to Lala on Thanksgiving. I asked her to let you know if there was something to tell and left it at that. You know I don't like getting in the middle of your personal business, but I guess there was something for her to tell you after all."

I smirked.

"Yeah I guess so."

"So how you feel about it, bro? What did you say when she told you?"

"I told her that shit sounded mighty convenient. She's been walking around knowing she was pregnant with my baby and didn't say shit to me until she's trying to guilt me into letting Marcus live," I said. "Shit sounds suspect as fuck."

"Bruh, I know you didn't just say that shit to her and leave," Nick said.

I raised my beer to my lips again, but Nick pulled it from my hand.

"Bruh, what the fuck?" he asked.

I just stared at him.

"Y'all have been creeping around and doing what y'all been doing all these years, and when you finally have a chance to be together for real this is what you do? She just shared some big news with you."

"And I just told her I'm gonna kill the last blood relative she has a connection to. There ain't no coming back from that."

Nick shook his head at me.

"Nah man. Ain't no coming back for y'all if you don't take your ass back over there and make this right," Nick said. "That's your woman, bruh. You love her, and we know she loves you more than Courtney ever did. Yeah ... Marcus is probably going to die, but she still has another blood relative – the baby that she's carrying. Your baby. You gotta fix this shit man."

I pinched the bridge of my nose and shook my head. My little brother was right. I stood up from my seat.

"Alright man. Let me get outta here. I'mma hit you up tomorrow," I said, slapping hands with him.

It had gotten late, but Nick was right. I needed to get home to my woman. I left his place and drove straight home. I pulled up a little before three in the morning and let myself in. I climbed the steps quietly and entered the darkened bedroom. Alana lay in the bed on her side with her back towards me like usual. I couldn't tell if she was sleeping or not. What I could see was that she had changed into an oversized T-shirt, pulled her hair into a bun, and I assume she had cried her way through the box of tissues scattered on her bedside table. I kicked off my shoes and stripped down to my T-shirt and underwear before getting into the bed and sliding close to her.

I felt her body tense, but she didn't turn to look at me.

"Why are you here?" she asked.

"Because I fucked up earlier, and I need to make it right."

"So, you're not going to kill my brother?"

I didn't respond. Alana pulled away from me and scooted closer to the edge of our bed.

"I didn't come home to talk about Marcus," I said, pulling her body back towards mine. "I'm talking about the way I reacted when you told me that we're having a baby. I need to apologize."

Alana didn't respond. She wasn't going to make my apology easy for me, but I didn't blame her. There was no excuse for the way I had spoken to her.

"I'm sorry, baby. The way I responded was wrong. I didn't mean to accuse you of lying or being manipulative ... none of that."

I paused for a moment.

"I was just fucked up about all the other stuff going on, but this isn't about that. This is about us ... and our baby. Lala, I meant what I said long ago when I told you that I got you. I got us, baby. There's nothing standing in our way now."

"But there is," she said softly.

She hadn't turned around to face me, but I could tell she was crying again.

"You're right, Lorenzo. I understand the game. I know what's going to happen to Marcus, and you're right. Even though I know how shit goes, I don't know if I could ever forgive you for that. If I can't forgive you, I don't see how we can be together."

I frowned.

"What are you saying, La?"

"I'm saying that if you kill my brother, we won't be able to get past that. There won't be a you and me. There probably won't be a baby either."

"What?" I quickly asked with a frown. She still refused to look at me. "Are you trying to tell me that you would get an abortion?"

"You need to decide what's more important to you ... starting a family with me or revenge," Alana answered.

I pulled away from her, rolling onto my back while I glared at the ceiling. My jaw was clenched tight.

"La ... that's not fair. What you're asking ..."

"What I'm asking is for you to make a choice and decide what matters to you more," she said. "You can't have both. You either get revenge, or you get me. You have to choose."

We laid in the silent darkness of our bedroom for what felt like an eternity. I wasn't sure I could agree to what she was asking.

"Are you telling me that you would really –"

"I've got a number for a private clinic saved in my phone right now," she responded.

I couldn't believe that she had already looked at abortion clinics. I continued to stare at the ceiling, shaking my head slowly. If I killed her brother, she would never forgive me. If I stood by and let my rage cause her to abort our baby, I wouldn't forgive myself. A few more moments of silence passed between us before I turned back on my side and reached for her again. I pulled Alana's body against mine, wrapping my arm around her waist and holding her close.

"Lala, I'm always going to choose you and our family," I said, kissing her cheek.

"I need to hear you say it."

I sighed.

"I'm not gonna lay a hand on him."

"Promise me."

"I promise, baby. I promise."

Alana didn't respond, but I finally felt her relax in my embrace. I continued to hold her close until I eventually heard the change in her breathing pattern. She had stopped crying and fell asleep. However, I couldn't close my eyes. My mind was racing a mile a minute. I had waited years for this opportunity with Alana. Everything within me wanted to build a life and a family with the woman I held in my arms ... but I couldn't let the situation with Marcus go. I had promised that I wouldn't kill her brother, but there had to be some sort of consequence. I was going to make sure of it.

𝕊 19 𝕊

ALANA

I couldn't help the smile that came to my face when I looked around the main floor of my house. It was Christmas evening, and Zo and I had a house full of friends and family. After we spent the morning alone eating breakfast and exchanging gifts, Zo and I went our separate ways for a few hours. While I went by Porsha's parents' home, he spent time with Courtney and the twins opening gifts. He returned home in time to welcome our guests. I was thankful that he had taken the lead on planning the evening in order to ensure I had a memorable and enjoyable Christmas. Our catered dinner was finished, and we were enjoying the company of those who had joined us.

I curled up on an accent chair near the fireplace, covering myself with a throw blanket while I watched Zo play spades with JB, Nick, and their cousin, Paul. Holiday music played in the background while others enjoyed conversation, television and other games. Nick and Zo's parents were there as well as Kayla, Lauren, Porsha, a few other guys Nick and Zo worked with, a couple of stylists from the salon, and Kiara and the girls. As perfect as the evening had been, I felt like there was one thing missing. I pulled out my cell phone and sent my brother another text message asking where he was. I tried to get in contact with him multiple times throughout the day, but he had not responded.

Shaking my head, I sighed but looked up from my phone when Zo's mother, Evelyn, sat down in the accent chair next to mine. She smiled at me.

"I thought you might want this. It's been a crowd favorite tonight, so I grabbed you a piece before it was all gone."

She handed me a piece of her homemade pound cake. She was right. Even though I was stuffed from dinner, I absolutely wanted the cake. Growing up, Evelyn was known around the neighborhood for her baking skills, and I had tasted plenty of her recipes. I took a big bite of the cake.

"Delicious like always," I said with a wide smile and a mouth full.

"Aww you've always been so sweet," she said as she patted my knee. "That's why I'm glad that knucklehead son of mine finally came to his senses."

I almost choked on my cake and looked at Evelyn with wide eyes. She laughed quietly while I struggled to swallow.

"Honey, he's had a thing for you since you all were younger. I knew how he felt about you the first time he brought you by the house. I could see it in his eyes. I don't know what he ever saw in Courtney. I love my grandbabies, but I'm glad that nightmare is finally over," she said. She leaned closer to me and said, "Courtney was never the one, sweetie. You are. I really hope he doesn't mess this up."

Evelyn gave me another warm smile before walking away and joining her husband, Zo and Nick's father, Brian, in the dining room. Zo glanced in my direction, winking at me before he turned his attention back to his card game. Porsha made her way across the room with a red Solo cup in her hand and sat down in the chair Evelyn occupied moments earlier. She raised the cup to her lips and took a big sip.

"Rum and coke?" I asked.

Porsha shook her head. "Something lighter. Sangria," she

answered. She looked at my near empty plate. "You keep eating like that, and everyone is going to know your secret."

I laughed. I had only gained a little weight with the pregnancy, but my pants were definitely starting to fit tighter.

"It's not going to be a secret for much longer. We're hovering around the end of the first trimester. As long as all is well at my next appointment, we plan to tell everyone pretty soon."

"The purchase of the salon will be complete soon too. A new business and a new baby. This is all so exciting," Porsha said with a wide smile. She looked past me. "Speaking of exciting ... your brother just got here with his fine self."

"What?"

I looked towards my front door to see Marcus standing in the foyer. I was glad he showed up, but there was an uneasy look on my face. He and Zo had not been in contact since Zo discovered the truth about his involvement in PO's death. Noticing the look on my face, Zo's smile dropped as he looked over his shoulder in the direction of the front door. After laying eyes on Marcus, he turned back towards me with his jaw tight. I avoided Zo's eye contact and quickly got up from my seat. I sat my empty cake plate down on a nearby table and headed towards my brother.

I was honestly surprised to see him. He had not responded to my attempts to reach him that day, and our communication had been strained since I found out what he had done. To the best of my knowledge he had not been in contact with Zo at all. I thought it was very bold of him to show up at a time when he knew Zo would be there.

"Hey! I didn't think I was going to see you when I didn't hear back from you," I said as I reached him.

Marcus took his coat off and hung it in the closet. "Sorry I didn't respond to your calls and texts. I've been a little busy."

He pulled me into a tight hug.

"Merry Christmas sister," he said. "Nice little gathering

you're having here. I'm glad I stopped by. I hope Mama Lacey made a cake."

Marcus released me from our hug and tried to head for the common area. I grabbed his arm and pulled him back towards me.

"Wait."

Marcus frowned.

"What's the problem?"

"I think you know what the problem is, Marcus. JB ... Nick ... Zo ... they're all here, and they know what you did," I said quietly. "When I texted you about coming over earlier in the day ... that was before everyone was here ... when Zo went to see the twins. I'm not sure that it's a good time for you to be here."

Marcus smiled and pulled my hand off his arm.

"Relax, La. Your boyfriend's not going to shoot me in the middle of your house, especially not on Christmas," he said.

Marcus turned away from me and was face to face with Zo. Standing in the foyer, I silently hoped and prayed that we didn't catch the attention of our houseguests.

"You said I'm not going to do what?" Zo questioned with a tight jaw.

The look in his eyes was daring Marcus to challenge him again. Marcus laughed and shook his head at Zo. Noticing a change in Zo's demeanor that typically meant trouble for whoever was on the receiving end of his rage, I stepped between the two men and placed a hand on Zo's chest, gently pushing him back a step.

"Marcus, don't taunt him. If you want to come by and spend the holiday with family, cool ... but you're only standing here because Zo made a promise to me that he wouldn't kill you," I said. "You might still have a problem with our relationship, but it's the only thing that saved your life."

"Oh yeah?" Marcus asked.

"That and the fact that I'm pregnant ... which is the main reason I asked him to spare you. You fucked up big time with what you did, but I want you to be around to meet your niece or nephew."

Marcus smirked and looked past me towards Zo.

"Guess I wasted energy being mad at you for breaking the code," he said. "I suppose I should have been thanking you this whole time for fucking my sister behind my back."

Zo started towards Marcus, and I struggled to keep them separated. Ignoring my brother's ignorance, I turned my attention towards Zo, who had fire in his eyes. The situation had the potential to go very badly very quickly.

"Remember what you promised me," I said, firmly holding on to his well-formed biceps.

I needed Marcus to stop talking. Zo was strong and towered over me. I knew that I would not be able to stop him if he really wanted to get at my brother. Zo continued to glare at Marcus instead of looking at me, but he didn't try to attack him. The commotion started to grab the attention of a few of our guests, and I noticed a few people casually glancing in our direction. Marcus laughed again.

"I highly doubt you want smoke with me with a house full of people on Christmas. You should listen to your girl, Big Guy," he said, patting Zo on the shoulder.

Marcus pushed past us on his way into the house, intentionally bumping into Zo in the process. As expected, Zo reacted. If I hadn't jumped in the way, I'm sure he would have tackled my brother in the middle of the great room. I had no idea why Marcus had shown up if he was going to be a complete asshole. Marcus and I both knew that he should have been killed just like the other people that were responsible for PO's murder. I damn near risked my relationship to save his life, and he was about to ruin our holiday.

"Hey! Babe ... look at me," I said to Zo, rubbing the side of his face. "You know he's an ass. Don't let that ruin our night."

Zo lowered his eyes to meet mine, but the anger was still present, and his jaw was still tight.

"I'm going to step out for a minute."

"Zo ... really?" I asked.

He grabbed his coat and keys.

"If he leaves before I get back, let me know," Zo said. "Otherwise, I'll see you later. Tell my folks and Nick."

I nodded. Maybe Zo stepping out for a minute was best for everybody. If Marcus continued to try him, I was sure they would come to blows again. Zo slipped into his coat, kissed me on the cheek, and walked out of the door. I hesitated for a moment before forcing a pleasant smile on my face and heading back to my chair.

ZO

I pulled into the garage a little before one in the morning. According to a text message from Alana, the house had cleared out about an hour prior. As bad as I felt about leaving her at the house alone, I knew that I needed to clear my head somewhere far away from her brother. I entered the house to see that the only light on the ground level came from the Christmas tree and there were very few signs of the party that remained. I hoped that someone helped Alana clean. I would feel terrible if I found out she had picked up by herself.

I jogged up the stairs to our bedroom to find Alana coming out of the bathroom dressed for bed. I smiled at her while she crossed the room to climb into the bed. Her plaid flannel pajama pants sat low on her hips and the tight tank top she wore displayed her small baby bump. It might have gone unnoticed by most other people. They probably would have assumed that she was eating a little too well during the holiday season.

"Did you do all that cleaning by yourself?"

She shook her head while she slid under the covers of our bed. "No. Your parents helped before they took off," she answered. "They want you to call them in the morning."

I nodded and stripped down to my underclothes before

climbing in the bed next to her. I wrapped an arm around her shoulders while Alana snuggled up to me, resting her head on my chest.

"Are you okay now?"

"Yeah," I answered, rubbing her shoulder. "Sorry about leaving like that. I didn't mean to run out on you, but –"

Alana shook her head. "You don't have to explain. I understand," she said. "I can't believe Marcus came in here the way he did after dodging the both of us for over a week."

"You know exactly why he was dodging me," I mumbled.

Alana sighed heavily. "Yeah, baby. I know."

There was a hint of sadness in her voice that caused me to sigh as well. I placed a hand on her stomach, softly caressing her bump. I silently reminded myself to hide my frustration with her brother when I was with her. I made a promise to her that I was not going to touch her brother, and I planned to stay true to my word. However, earlier in the evening while I was riding around, trying to clear my mind, a thought occurred to me. I knew that Marcus needed to pay for his actions, and I discovered that there was a way to make that happen and keep my promise to Alana. The way things currently stood; Marcus was the dark cloud hanging over our relationship. I had to make him disappear, but in the meantime, I decided to change the subject.

"Other than that bullshit with your brother, did you enjoy your Christmas?"

Alana nodded. "I did. I really did. Thank you for everything."

"It was worth it to see the smile on your face."

Alana smiled at me before resting her head on my chest again. In a matter of minutes, she fell asleep, snoring lightly. I would be awake for a few more hours, holding her close and watching basketball highlights on ESPN. From the moment I started working for Julian Reid when I was fifteen years old, I knew that things could change at the drop of a dime. There had been so much commotion in my life personally and professionally over the last five years that I made sure to enjoy the moments of peace and quiet whenever I could. Lying in bed with my woman on Christmas night felt like the calm before the storm, and I was determined to live in the moment.

Two days later, I walked into McCormick & Schmick's to meet Mayor Richardson for a late lunch. The hostess led me to a secluded table where the mayor was already waiting.

"Mr. Lacey, always a pleasure to see you," Mayor Richardson said while we shook hands.

"Likewise."

I sat down across from him and briefly glanced at the menu in front of me even though I didn't have much of an appetite. Our meeting was not a social visit. Mayor Richardson would play a vital part in how I planned to handle Marcus without personally laying hands on him. We engaged in several minutes of small talk and placed our food orders before getting to the real reason behind our meeting.

"So, what brings us here today?" Mayor Richardson asked. He took a sip of his drink and leaned back in his seat. "I enjoy our business discussions, but you normally give me status updates at the beginning of the month. We're a few days ahead of January, and your message said you had something important to discuss. Something that could affect business?"

I nodded. "Yeah. You know we've been looking into the circumstances surrounding PO's untimely death and individuals who may have been responsible."

"Of course. I believe you said that matter was handled already?"

I sighed heavily.

"That's what I thought."

Mayor Richardson's forehead wrinkled. "I'm assuming there is a new development?" he asked.

"There is," I answered. "Turns out someone else is responsible."

"Someone other than the crew of folks you and your people spent weeks tracking down?"

I nodded.

"Yes."

"Hmm ... and this other person has not been taken care of?"

"No."

Mayor Richardson sat up a little straighter in his chair. "So, I assume you think you need my help, and that's why we're here today," he said. I nodded, and he continued. "Well Lorenzo, I'm a little confused. It seems that taking care of things of that nature is more your area of expertise than mine. You wiped out an entire crew of people you *thought* were responsible with only one incident making a brief mention on the five o'clock news. Seems to me you know how to *fix* a problem like that all on your own. How can I possibly be of assistance?"

"The person responsible is actually a member of my team. Although I would very much like to handle them in the same way I handled the others, I can't."

"You can't?"

I shook my head. "No. I can't. Without getting into all the details, I just need you to know that it is important for the sake of business that this person is off the streets but still alive ... for the time being anyway."

Mayor Richardson nodded, and a knowing grin came to his face. He took another sip of his drink and leaned back in his seat again.

"I understand what you're saying now. That's definitely something I can help with, especially if you think keeping this person is going to be a problem for business. That's something you and I are definitely on the same page about. Neither one of us wants issues with that can affect our pockets. Things have been going so smoothly lately," he said. "How long do you need this person off the streets? Are you thinking a felony drug charge or something that's going to require a bit more time?"

"I need him gone for a while ... a long while"

Mayor Richardson nodded.

"Yes. I think I can definitely help you with that," he said with a slight smile. "I can handle that with a simple conversation. I just need a few details from you, and I can have this person off the streets in no time. Anything to help the business."

A genuine smile came to my face at the thought that I was going to be able to take care of Marcus without personally touching him myself.

"That's music to my ears. What all do you need to know?"

✸ 20 ✸
ALANA

"Okay, Alana. Let's take a listen to the baby's heartbeat," Dr. Whitfield said as she grabbed her fetal doppler.

I leaned back on the exam table and rolled my shirt up while my doctor reached for the ultrasound gel. There was a light knock on the door before it pushed open slowly.

"Sorry I'm late," Zo said, entering the room and closing the door.

"Better late than never," Dr. Whitfield said with a smile, waving him over to the exam table. "You're actually just in time to hear the heartbeat."

Zo locked eyes with me, and we smiled at each other as he approached the table. He stood beside me while Dr. Whitfield squeezed the cold gel onto my stomach. A few moments later, the silence in the room was filled with the loud racing sound of the baby's heartbeat. Zo's smile widened before he kissed my forehead. Dr. Whitfield looked at her watch to ensure a full minute passed before turning the machine off.

"One hundred and fifty-five," she said with a smile of her own. "Very good. Very strong."

She sat the doppler down on the counter. Zo helped me sit

up while Dr. Whitfield sat down on her stool and looked over the notes on her laptop.

"I assume this is dad?" she asked looking up at me.

I nodded.

"Perfect," she said. "I want to go over the bloodwork we did the last time you were here. We did a couple of screenings since we don't have a good family medical history for you, Alana."

I nodded. Although it made me anxious, I agreed to the extra testing. I was hopeful all would be fine, but the truth was that I had no idea about my family's medical history. That was all due to a deceased, drug addicted mother and a father I never knew. Sensing my uneasiness, Zo reached for my hand while Dr. Whitfield looked back down at her laptop.

"Everything looks pretty good," Dr. Whitfield said. "I don't see anything here for you two to be concerned about. We're right at the end of the first trimester, and the heart rate is so strong. Alana, I think you can relax and breathe a little easier."

Dr. Whitfield looked back up at me, and I smiled in her direction.

"There's one other thing," she said. "We were able to determine the baby's gender from the bloodwork. Are you interested in finding out today? We can also wait until a later visit or the delivery room. Whatever you two decide."

I looked at Zo, and he shrugged his shoulders.

"Whatever you want, La. I already know it's going to be another boy," he joked.

I rolled my eyes at him and laughed.

"Dr. Whitfield, we can find out today," I told her.

"Okay. You two are expecting a little baby girl," she said with a wide smile.

"A girl?" I asked.

"Yes ma'am. A baby girl. The bloodwork we did ..."

Dr. Whitfield explained the science behind the bloodwork, and how she was able to make a determination at an early stage. While I tuned her out, becoming lost in my own thoughts, I looked at Zo who was staring at Dr. Whitfield and hanging on to her every word. I was still in awe that this was actually happening. We were having a child. Zo had already demonstrated the type of father he was when it came to his twins. I couldn't wait to see how he was going to be with his baby girl.

I turned my attention back to Dr. Whitfield nodding appropriately when needed as she went over the last few details and confirmed our appointment for the following month. After the doctor left the room, Zo helped me down from the exam table. I slipped into my jacket and grabbed my purse.

"Sorry I was a little late," he said. "I met with the divorce attorney first thing this morning. Then I got a little tied up with work, but I'm free for the rest of the day. I'm all yours."

I smiled at him while retrieving my keys from my coat pocket.

"You hungry?" Zo asked. He checked the time. "We can grab a late lunch or something."

I shook my head. "No. I ate before I came here," I said. "I really just want to go home. I was on my feet most of the day. I just want to lay in the bed and watch TV."

"Works for me," Zo said, as he opened the door and we stepped into the hallway. "Whatever you want."

"Whatever I want, huh?" I asked with a smile. I headed towards the front door with Zo following close behind me. "A girl could get used to that type of treatment."

Zo laughed and shook his head. We started across the parking lot to our vehicles.

"La, quit playing," he said. "You've always gotten whatever you wanted from me, and now you're carrying my baby girl so that shit's only gonna to get worse. I'm bout to spoil the hell out of y'all. Forever."

"Forever, huh?"

A smile tugged at my lips. I turned around, leaning against my driver door to look into Zo's face. He nodded.

"Hell yeah, baby. Forever."

Zo placed his hands on my waist and kissed my lips.

He pulled away and said, "Now let's go home and get in the bed."

MARCUS

I yawned and stretched my arms while I sat up in my bed and scooted towards the edge. I shook my head when I noticed it was completely dark outside. Since it was still winter, I knew it could be anywhere between six in the evening and six in the morning. I picked up my phone to check the time. It was a little before seven at night. I released a heavy sigh. What was supposed to be a quick nap had turned into me sleeping through the rest of the afternoon. I wasted my day sleeping, but there was work to take care of that night.

I stood up from the bed and stretched again. Fumbling around in the dark, I turned on the nearest lamp and looked towards my bedside table when I heard my phone vibrate. Porsha was calling me.

"What's good?"

"Nothing much," she answered. "Just getting ready for Alana's dinner party. Am I going to see you tonight?"

I ran a hand over my face trying to fully wake up.

"I'm not gonna be at the dinner, but if you want to come through later just hit me up."

Porsha hesitated.

"Or don't," I said shrugging my shoulders.

Porsha and I had been messing around off and on since I got home, but the situation wasn't that deep to me.

"What? No that's not why I paused. I want to see you tonight."

"Then what's the problem?"

"It's no problem, Marcus. I just ... I just thought you would be over this whole thing with Alana and Zo by now. You've always been there for her. Buying the salon is a big deal. I can't believe you're not going to help her celebrate that," Porsha said. She sighed heavily. "I just thought y'all would be able to put the bullshit to the side tonight."

I released a heavy sigh of my own. Porsha thought the tension between Zo, Alana, and I still stemmed from their relationship. I was surprised that Alana had not told her the truth about PO. The two had been best friends forever. They shared everything.

"Well you thought wrong," I said. "I'm not going to her dinner, because I wasn't invited."

"Oh. I – I didn't know that," Porsha stuttered. "I –"

"It's cool," I said. "I'm not sweating it. Go on to her little party and have fun. I'll talk to you later."

"Marcus, I –"

"Porsha, it's cool. I gotta go anyway. I'll talk to you later."

I hung up the phone before she could say anything else. I grabbed my keys and coat and headed for the front door. Although Zo was aware of my involvement in PO's death, business had continued as usual. There was obvious tension between me and the team, but thanks to my sister I didn't have to fear for my life. I was able to keep making money and minding my business because she had Zo's nose so wide open that he actually promised he wouldn't kill me.

I shook my head and laughed at the thought. I never would have predicted it. That crazy ass nigga was getting soft.

I left my apartment and made my way to the Altima. It was a Friday night. I was headed to the weekly handoff. Zo's system was so efficient that I knew I wouldn't be there long. I anticipated hearing from Porsha after she left Alana's dinner party. We would probably be clear around the same time.

After a fifteen-minute drive, I pulled off of the interstate onto a side street. I was only a few minutes away from the spot. As I approached a traffic light, I made the decision to continue through the intersection on a yellow light. A split second later, I saw the flashing lights behind me. I sighed heavily.

"Shit," I mumbled under my breath.

I pulled over to the side and put the car in park while I waited for the officer to approach me. It would be a minor inconvenience, but I was not too worried about being pulled over. I never drove solo in my sister's car with any guns or drugs. That night wasn't any different. I knew there would be an extra gun amongst the crew if needed.

Several minutes later, the officer approached the vehicle asking for my license and registration. He appeared professional and cordial enough. He claimed that he pulled me over because I ran a red light. I knew that was a lie, but I also knew better than to argue with Atlanta Police over something as simple as a moving violation. I just wanted to get the ticket so I could continue on to my destination. However, the longer I waited for the officer to return with my license, the more I started to think that there was some other problem I didn't know about. I shook my head in disbelief when a few more patrol cars pulled up with flashing lights. He had waited for backup.

I watched in the mirrors while the officer with my license spoke with one of the officers that just arrived. After a short conversation, they approached the car – one on each side of the vehicle and both had their hands on their service weapons.

"Mr. Woods, I'm going to need for you to step out of the vehicle for me," the first officer said calmly.

I frowned.

"Why?"

"Sir, we have probable cause to search the vehicle due to the suspicious smell of marijuana," the officer stated.

"Yeah okay."

I shook my head at the officer but followed his instructions. There may have been a faint smell of marijuana from a blunt I smoked earlier in the day, but again – I knew there wasn't anything illegal in the car. As I stepped out of the vehicle, the officer put me in handcuffs and instructed me to sit on the curb while he and his partner searched the vehicle. I sat on the curb growing more and more irritated by the second but forced myself to remain calm. I had a long history of run-ins with law enforcement. I was prepared for their bullshit.

But I wasn't prepared for what I saw when the second officer opened the car door to start looking through the vehicle. Underneath the driver's seat, I saw the handle of a nickel-plated 40 caliber pistol right before the first officer pulled it from underneath my seat. When he held it up to inspect it, I shook my head in disbelief. I recognized the gun, but it wasn't mine. The second officer, the one closest to where I sat, pulled me up to my feet. The officer gave me my Miranda rights while he led me to the patrol car. While the second officer guided me into the back-seat and closed the door, I watched while the first officer bagged the gun – the unlicensed, unregistered weapon that I knew belonged to Zo. The same weapon I knew he used to kill Tank. I was being arrested for illegal possession of a firearm by a convicted felon, but I knew that a murder charge was coming soon. I had Zo to thank for that.

I should have known better.

Sure, he had promised my sister that he wouldn't kill me. I guess she didn't make him promise that there wouldn't be any revenge at all. This was his way of getting rid of me without putting me six feet under. Clever. He always was the one with the brains. He was able to get to me before I could get to him.

Well played, I thought while the officer started towards the precinct. *Well played*.

TO BE CONTINUED ...

ACKNOWLEDGMENTS

As always, thank you to my family and closest friends. You all have been in my corner encouraging me from the beginning. Collectively, you gave me confidence to share my stories with the world. You all mean everything to me.

To everyone who has read any of my work, thank you! It still feels surreal to get emails from readers asking when the next book is coming out, but I love all the support and interactions. Let's stay connected because more books are on the way!

ABOUT THE AUTHOR

Michelle Elaine is an author of African American and Urban fiction and romance. Born and raised in Atlanta, GA, she still resides in the metro area with her husband and sons. She has always been passionate about storytelling and character creation/development. This passion led to several short stories and development of plots and characters before she completed her first book, "A Good Girl & A Down South Millionaire". Visit her website and join her mailing list to stay in the know on the latest releases, etc.

Other ways to stay connected:
    Facebook – Author Michelle Elaine
    Instagram – authormichelleelaine
    Website – www.michelleelainebooks.com
    Email – michelleelainebooks@outlook.com